WE'RE FAILURES

We were supposed to be this super setup to make the Constitution work. Everyone would have their freedoms while the destructive elements were put in their place.

"Yes," said Smith.

"What do you mean 'yes'?" said Remo. "We were a fucking waste of time! We had a president who would have been convicted of breaking and entering if he didn't get a pardon. Half the top government is in jail, the other half ought to be. You can't walk in the city streets unless you know how to kill. You read every day where this cop and that is on the take. Care for the aged has turned into a gigantic ripoff. And all this while I'm up to my armpits in bodies, supposedly ending this sort of crap."

"That's just what CURE is doing," said Smith.

"And what you're seeing, Remo, is the organization finally working. This is the pus coming out of the lanced boil. Remo, just how do you think we work? You're seeing this country do what no other democracy has been able to do. We're cleaning house."

"Why didn't I know about this?"

"Because we only use you for emergencies. You're what I use when things go wrong or can't go right any other way . . ."

THE DESTROYER
By Warren Murphy and Richard Sapir

Available wherever paperbacks are sold, or order direct from the Publisher. Send cover price plus 50¢ per copy for mailing and handling to Pinnacle Books, Dept. 17-23, 475 Park Avenue South, New York, N.Y. 10016. Residents of New York, New Jersey and Pennsylvania must include sales tax. DO NOT SEND CASH.

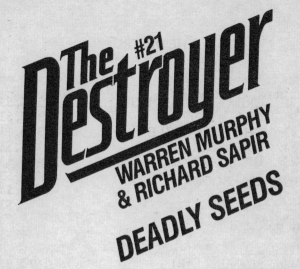

The #21
Destroyer

WARREN MURPHY
& RICHARD SAPIR

DEADLY SEEDS

PINNACLE BOOKS
WINDSOR PUBLISHING CORP.

PINNACLE BOOKS

are published by

Windsor Publishing Corp.
475 Park Avenue South
New York, NY 10016

Seventh printing: June 1989

Printed in the United States of America

For Derek Cross
—my favorite pessimist

DEADLY SEEDS

CHAPTER ONE

When James Orayo Fielding looked at people, he saw
bugs. Except bugs didn't cry or quiver or try to hide
their terror when he fired them or told them he might
fire them. Bugs went squish when he stepped on them.
And then his manservant Oliver would clean up the little blotches with his thumbnail and James Orayo Fielding would ask:

"Don't you hate that, Oliver? Doesn't it make your
stomach turn to put your fingers in a bug's belly?"

And Oliver would say:

"No, Mr. Fielding. My job is to do whatever you
wish."

"What if I told you to eat it, Oliver?"

"Then I would do as you wish, Mr. Fielding."

"Eat it, Oliver."

And James Orayo Fielding would watch very closely
and inspect Oliver's hands to make sure he hadn't
pushed a remnant of the insect up into his sleeve, or
in some other manner deceived his employer.

1

"People are bugs, Oliver."

"Yes, Mr. Fielding."

"I'll wear grays today."

"Yes, Mr. Fielding."

And James Orayo Fielding waited by the immense picture window that gave him the glorious view of the Rocky Mountains, stretching in white peaks right to Canada and left to Mexico. The Fieldings were one of the old Denver, Colorado, families, descended from English nobility on the father's side and French on the mother's, although it was rumored some Arapaho had made its way into the bloodstream, culminating in James Orayo Fielding, owner of the Fielding ranches, Fielding sugar beet plants, and Fielding Enterprises Inc., which included manufacturing plants in New Mexico and Texas which few Denverites knew anything about. James did not discuss them.

Oliver knelt as he held out the soft gray flannel pants for Mr. Fielding to step into. He fitted the Italian shoes over Mr. Fielding's feet, then the broadcloth white shirt, tied the black and orange stripes of Princeton around Mr. Fielding's neck, slipped the Phi Beta Kappa key into Mr. Fielding's gray vest, and buttoned the vest down to Mr. Fielding's belt. The gray jacket went on over the vest and Oliver brought the mirror for inspection. It was full length and silver-framed and rolled on wheels to the center of Mr. Fielding's dressing room.

Fielding looked at himself, a man in his early forties, without gray in his temples, full soft brown hair which Oliver now combed to that casual neatness, a patrician countenance with delicate straight nose, an honest-man's mouth, and a gentle cool in his blue eyes. He formed a sincere involved expression with his face, and

2

thought to himself that that expression would be just fine.

He used it that afternoon in El Paso when he told union negotiators that he was closing down Fielding Conduit and Cable Inc.

"The costs, gentlemen, just don't allow me to continue operations."

"But you can't do that," said the union negotiator. "There are 456 families that depend on Fielding Conduit and Cable for their existence."

"You don't think I'd close down a factory just to watch 456 families wriggle and squirm, do you?" asked Fielding, using the expression he had practiced earlier in the day in his Denver home. "If you wish, gentlemen, I will explain it to your membership in person."

"You'd stand up in front of our membership and tell them they're all out of jobs? In an economy like today?" asked the union negotiator, trembling. He lit a cigarette while one burned unfinished in the ashtray. Fielding watched it.

"Yes, yes, I would," said Fielding. "And I think you should bring the families too."

"Sir," said the corporation counsel for Fielding Conduit and Cable. "You don't have to do that. It's not your responsibility. It's the union's job."

"I want to," said Fielding.

"What if we took a pay cut?" asked the union negotiator. "An across-the-board pay cut?"

"Hmmm," said Fielding and had the company's profit-and-loss statement brought to him. "Hmmm. Maybe," said Fielding after examining the printed sheet.

"Yes? Yes?" said the union negotiator.

"Maybe. Just maybe," said Fielding.

3

"Yes!" said the union negotiator.

"We could use the factory itself to inform the families we're closing. You can get them together in two hours, can't you? I know almost the entire membership is down at the union hall."

"I guess we could do that," said the negotiator, crushed.

"Maybe in two hours, I can work out something. Okay?"

"What?" said the negotiator, suddenly revived.

"I'm not sure yet," said Fielding. "Tell them it looks as if we're going to shut down but I may work out something by this evening."

"I've got to know what, Mr. Fielding. I can't raise their hopes without something concrete."

"Well, then, don't raise their hopes," said Fielding and left with his corporation counsel for dinner in a small El Paso restaurant he favored. They dined on clams *oreganato,* lobster *fra diavolo,* and a warm runny custard called *zabaglione.* Fielding showed his corporation counsel pictures he had taken of the famine in India as part of his famine study for the Denver chapter of Cause, a worldwide relief agency.

His meal ruined, the corporation counsel asked Fielding what he gave one of the children he saw, a child with protruding ribs, hollow eyes and starvation thick belly.

"A fiftieth at f/4.5 on Plus-X film," said Fielding, dunking the crisp golden crust of fresh-baked Italian bread into the spicy red tomato sauce of his lobster *fra diavolo*. "Aren't you going to eat your *scungilli?*"

"No. No. Not now," said the lawyer.

"Well, considering the starvation in the world, you ought to be ashamed of yourself wasting food. Eat."

4

"I—I—"

"Eat," ordered Fielding. And he watched to make sure his corporation counsel ate every last bit of his dinner for the sake of the starving children in India whose pictures he left displayed on the table.

"Look," he said. "I'm suffering too. I've had stomach pains for weeks. Going to see my doctor tonight back in Denver. But I'm eating."

"You're going home tonight?" said the lawyer. "Then you don't have a plan for the workers?"

"I do have a plan. In a way," said Fielding.

When they arrived at the factory, the low white-washed building was lit and buzzing with families packed lathe to drill press. Children stuck fingers in lathes and mothers yanked them back. Union men talked among themselves in that low choppy talk of men who know that all has been said and anything more is a waste of time. Their lives were out of their hands.

When Fielding entered, the main factory building hushed as if someone had turned simultaneous dials in nearly a thousand throats. One child laughed and the laughter stopped with a loud motherly smack.

Fielding led four white-coated men wheeling carts with round tubs on them to a raised podium in front of the factory. Smiling, he took the microphone from the nervous union negotiator.

"I've got good news for you all tonight," he said and nearly five hundred families exploded in cheers and applause. Husbands hugged wives. Some wept. One woman kept yelling, "God bless you, Mr. Fielding," and she was heard when the cheering subsided and that energized more cheering. Fielding waited with a big warm smile on his face, his right hand tucked into his

5

gray vest, safe from the grubby reachings of union officials. The corporation counsel waited by the door, looking at his feet.

Fielding raised both arms and was given quiet.

"As I said when I was interrupted, I have good news for you tonight. You see the gentlemen with white coats. You see the tubs on the carts. Ladies and gentlemen, children, union officials, there's free ice cream tonight. For everyone."

A woman up front looked to her husband and asked if she had heard correctly. In the back row families buzzed in confusion. At the door, the corporation counsel blew air out of his mouth and stared at the ceiling.

Fielding assumed the sincere concerned expression he had perfected earlier in the day before the silver-framed full-length mirror in his dressing room.

"That's the good news. Now the bad news. There is no way we can continue operations of Fielding Conduit and Cable."

At a main lathe fifty yards back, a middle-aged man in a red checked jacket cleared his throat. Everyone heard him.

"Ow," said the union negotiator. And everyone heard him too.

Fielding nodded to a white-jacketed busboy that he might start serving the ice cream. The boy looked at the crowd and shook his head.

A man in the front row jumped up onto his seat. His wife tried to tug him back down but he freed the arm she held.

"You ever own a plant in Taos, New Mexico?" yelled the man.

"Yes," said Fielding.

"And did you shut down that one too?"

"We had to," said Fielding.

"Yeah. I thought so. I heard about this ice cream trick you pulled in Taos. Just like tonight."

"Gentlemen, my counsel will explain everything shortly," said Fielding and leaped from the little platform at the front of the factory and made his way quickly to the door before the rush of workers could get at him.

"Tell them about our tax structure," yelled Fielding, pushing his lawyer between himself and the surging workers and just making it out the door. He ran to the car and made a leisurely mental note that he should phone the El Paso police to rescue the lawyer. Yes, he would call. From his doctor's office in Denver.

At the airport, Oliver was waiting in the Lear jet. It had been checked out and readied by airport mechanics.

"Everything turn out satisfactorily, sir?" asked Oliver, holding out the suede flying jacket.

"Perfectly," said James Orayo Fielding, not telling his manservant about the stabbing pains in his stomach. Why give Oliver any joy?

If he did not have the appointment that evening, he would have taken the slower Cessna twin-engine prop job. With that one, he could leave the fuselage door open and watch Oliver clutch his seat as the wind whipped at his face. Once, during an Immelman turn, Oliver had passed out in the Cessna. When Fielding saw this, he leveled the plane and undid Oliver's safety strap. The manservant recovered, saw the unbuckled strap, and passed out again. James Orayo Fielding loved his old propeller plane.

Doctor Goldfarb's office on Holly Street shone like three white squares against a dark checkerboard of

7

black square windows. If any other patient had asked for this evening appointment, Dr. Goldfarb would have referred him to someone else. But it was James Orayo Fielding who had asked for that specific appointment to get the results of his every-six-months physical, and that meant that Fielding had no other free time. And what else could be expected of a man so fully occupied with the world's welfare? Wasn't Mr. Fielding chairman of the Denver chapter of Cause? Hadn't he personally visited India, Bangladesh, the Sahel to see famine first-hand and come back to Denver to tell everyone about it?

Another man with Fielding's wealth might just have sat back and become a playboy. But not James Orayo Fielding. Where there was suffering, you would find James Orayo Fielding. So when Mr. Fielding said he was only free this one night of the month, Dr. Goldfarb told his daughter he would have to leave just after he gave her away at the wedding ceremony.

"Darling, I'll try to be back before the reception is over," he had told her. And that was the easy part. The hard part was what he was going to tell Mr. Fielding about the checkup. Like most doctors, he did not like telling a patient he was going to die. But with Mr. Fielding, it was like being part of a sin.

Fielding noticed immediately that the runty Dr. Goldfarb had trouble telling him something. So Fielding pressed him on it, and got the answer.

"A year to fifteen months," said Dr. Goldfarb.

"There's no operation possible?"

"An operation is useless. It's a form of anemia, Mr. Fielding. We don't know why it strikes when it strikes. It has nothing to do with your diet."

"And there's no cure?" asked Fielding.

8

"None."

"You know, of course, I feel it's my duty to myself to check other authorities."

"Yes, of course," said Dr. Goldfarb. "Of course."

"I think I'll find you correct however," said Fielding.

"I'm afraid you will," said Dr. Goldfarb and then he saw the most shocking thing from a terminal patient. Dr. Goldfarb had experienced hostility, denial, melancholy, and hysteria. But he had never seen before what he encountered now.

James Orayo Fielding grinned, a small controlled play of life at the corners of his mouth, a casual amusement.

"Dr. Goldfarb, bend over here," said Fielding, beckoning the doctor's ear with a wag of his forefinger.

"You know something?" he whispered.

"What?" Goldfarb asked.

"I don't give a shit."

As Fielding had expected, Dr. Goldfarb was right. In New York City he was proven right. In Zurich and Munich, in London and Paris, he was proven right, give or take a few months.

But it didn't matter because Fielding had devised a great plan, a plan worth a life.

His manservant Oliver watched him closely. Fielding had rented a DC-10 for their travels and turned the tail section into two small bedrooms. He took the seats out of the main section and installed two large working desks, a bank of small computers, and five teletype machines. Above the main working desk, Fielding had installed an electronic calendar that worked in reverse. The first day had read one year (inside) to fifteen months (outside). The second day of flight on the short hop from Zurich to Munich, it registered eleven months, twenty-nine days (inside) to fourteen months, twenty-nine days (outside). It was the countdown, Oliver realized, to what Mr. Fielding had called his termination.

As they left Munich, Oliver noticed two strange things. The outside date had been changed to eighteen months, and Mr. Fielding had Oliver shred a three-foot-high computer printout, which Fielding had studied for hours before angrily writing across the top: "Money is not enough."

"Good news, I trust, sir," said Oliver.

"You mean on the new outside date? Not really. I'm hardly even bothering myself with the outside date. What I've got to do has to be done within the inside date. The doctors in Munich said they had seen someone live eighteen months with this, so maybe I'll live eighteen months. You'd like that, wouldn't you, Oliver?"

"Yes, Mr. Fielding."

"You're a liar, Oliver."

"As you say, Mr. Fielding."

On a flight from London to New York City, Oliver was ordered to shred three days of teleprint from the teletypewriters that clacked incessantly in the main section. On top of the thick pile of papers, Fielding had written: "Chicago grain market not enough."

"Good news, I trust, sir," said Oliver.

"Any other man would give up at this point. But men are bugs, Oliver."

"Yes, Mr. Fielding."

In New York City, the plane stayed parked three days at the La Guardia Marine Air Terminal.

On the first day, Oliver shredded heavy reports

topped by Fielding's note reading: "The weather is not enough."

On the second day, Mr. Fielding hummed *Zippety Doo Da*. On the third day, he danced little steps between the computer and his desk, which had become a meticulously organized pile of charts and reports. A very thin manila envelope on top of the pile was labeled:

"ENOUGH."

Oliver opened it when Mr. Fielding bathed before dinner. He saw a single handwritten note.

"Needed: One average public relations agency, radioactive waste, construction crews, commodities analysts —and six months of life."

Oliver did not see the single small gray hair that had been atop the envelope. James Orayo Fielding did when he returned. The paper hair was now on the desk. It had been moved from where he had placed it on the envelope.

"Oliver," said Fielding, "we're flying home tonight."

"Should I inform the crew?"

"No," said Fielding. "I think I'd like to pilot myself."

"If I may suggest, sir, you're not checked out in a DC-10, sir."

"You're so right, Oliver. Right again. So bright. We will have to rent a Cessna."

"A Cessna, sir?"

"A Cessna, Oliver."

"The jet is faster, sir. We don't have to make stops."

"But not as much fun, Oliver."

"Yes, Mr. Fielding."

When the Cessna took off, a hot muggy summer

11

morning broke red over New York City, like a warm soot blanket. Oliver saw the sun through the open door to his left. He saw the runway leave underneath him and the houses become small. He smelled his own breakfast coming back up his throat and into his mouth, and he returned it to the world in a little paper bag he always brought with him when Mr. Fielding flew the Cessna. At five thousand feet, Oliver became faint and lay back limply as Mr. Fielding sang, "A tisket, A tasket, I found a yellow basket."

Over Harrisburg, Pennsylvania, Mr. Fielding spoke.

"I suppose you're wondering what I'm doing, Oliver," said Mr. Fielding. "As you know, I have eleven months, two weeks to live, inside date. Maybe even less. One can't trust the human body. To some, this would be a tragedy. Would it be a tragedy to you, Oliver?"

"What, Mr. Fielding?"

"Would death be a tragedy to you?"

"Yes sir."

"To me, Oliver, it's freedom. I am no longer bound to protect my image in Denver. Do you know why I cultivated my image in Denver, keeping my fun to El Paso and places like that?"

"No sir."

"Because the bugs crawl all over you if you're different, if you frighten them. Bugs hate anything better than them."

"Yes sir."

"Well, in a year, they can't get to me. And I'm going to get them first. More than Adolf Hitler or Joseph Stalin or Mao Tse-tung. I will get a million. A billion at least. Not millions. A billion. A billion bugs, Oliver. Me. I will do it. And none of them will be able to bother me again. Oliver, it will be beautiful."

12

"Yes sir."

"If you knew you were going to die, Oliver, would you stop saying 'yes sir' and say 'fuck you, Mr. Fielding'?"

"Never, sir."

"Let's see, Oliver."

And James Orayo Fielding snapped on his oxygen mask and brought the plane up to where he saw Oliver slump back, unconscious, and he reached behind himself and unsnapped Oliver's safety strap and put the twin-engine Cessna into a dive. Oliver flipped back out of his seat and was pressed by the force of gravity into the rear of the plane. When Fielding leveled the Cessna at three thousand feet, Oliver curled into a ball on the floor.

"Ohhh," he said, regaining consciousness. He lifted himself on his hands and as his head cleared and as he breathed more easily, he felt himself being pulled forward. Mr. Fielding had put the plane in a slight dive. And Oliver was going forward, toward the door on the left. Suddenly the plane banked left and Oliver was going out through the door. He grabbed the bottom bar of a seat and clutched.

"Mr. Fielding, Mr. Fielding! Help! Help!" he yelled, the air whipping at his midsection, the liquid of his bladder running out through his trousers.

"You may now say 'fuck you'," said Fielding.

"No sir," said Oliver.

"Well, then, don't say I didn't give you your chance. Goodbye, Oliver."

And the plane rolled farther to its left until Oliver was holding on to the seat, now above him, and as it cruised that way, Oliver felt his hands grown numb. Perhaps Mr. Fielding was just testing him, knew exactly how long it would take, and then would turn the plane aright and help him back in. Mr. Fielding was a peculiar sort, but not totally cruel. He wouldn't kill his manservant, Oliver. The plane snapped back abruptly over to its other side and Oliver found himself holding air, his body moving forward at the same speed as the plane, then downward. Very downward.

Oliver knew this because the plane appeared to be going up while flying level. And as Oliver spun, he saw the broad Pennsylvania country grow clearer and bigger beneath him. And it was coming towards him. He went beyond panic into that peace of dying men, where they understand that they are one with the universe, eternal with all life, the coming and going of one part of all that life, just a throb.

And Oliver saw the white and blue Cessna dive. And Mr. Fielding had come down to see Oliver's face. Mr. Fielding in a dive looking at Oliver, red-faced and yelling something. What was it? Oliver couldn't hear. He waved goodbye and smiled and said softly, "God bless you, Mr. Fielding."

Shortly thereafter, Oliver met a field of green summer corn.

James Orayo Fielding pulled up out of the dive still screaming.

"Yell 'fuck you'. Yell 'fuck you'. Yell 'fuck you'."

Fielding trembled at the controls. His hands were sweaty on the instruments. He felt his stomach heave. Oliver hadn't been a bug; he had shown incredible courage. What if Fielding were wrong about bugs? What if he were wrong about everything? He was going to be just as dead as Oliver. Nothing could save him.

By Ohio, Fielding wrested back control of himself. A momentary panic happened to everyone. He had

14

done the absolutely right thing. Oliver had to die. He had seen the plan, just as sure as hairs placed atop folders did not move by themselves.

Everything would work perfectly. Within eleven months, one week and six days.

(Inside).

CHAPTER TWO

His name was Remo and the hot Newark night offended him, and the smells from the alley where rats scratched inside open garbage cans filled his senses with decay and the occasional street lights cast more glare than illumination. It was summer and it was Newark, New Jersey, and he was never to come back to this city alive because he had left it dead.

This was where he was born. Down the street a large dark red brick building with broken glass shards in empty black frames stood surrounded by litter-heavy lots, waiting to become a lot itself. That was where he was raised. He used to say it was where he was educated until his real education began. That was where he was Remo Williams and the nuns taught him washing, bed-making, politeness, and that rulers on knuckles hurt when you were caught in violation. Later he would learn that punishment for sin was haphazard but the effects of sin were immediate. They told in your body and your breathing; they robbed you of proper-

16

ness, which could mean death. But the death was haphazard; the improperness itself was the real punishment. In this new life, the sins were panic and laziness, and the original sin was incompetence.

Remo thought of the ruler as he made out the old soot-covered concrete lettering above the boarded-up door:

"St. Theresa's Orphanage."

He would have liked to have seen Sister Mary Elizabeth now. Open up his hand for that ruler and let her flail away and laugh at her. He had tried by sheer willpower more than twenty years before. But Sister Mary Elizabeth knew her business better than Remo had known his. Smiles were not too convincing when your hand trembled and your eyes watered. But he didn't know then about pain. Now she could have used a kitchen knife and it wouldn't cut his flesh.

"You there," came a voice from behind him. Remo had heard the car move silently up the street. He glanced over his shoulder. A uniformed police sergeant, his face shiny from the sweat of night heat, leaned out the open squad car window. His hands were hidden. Remo knew he held a weapon. He was not sure how he knew. Perhaps it was the way the man held his body. Perhaps it was in the man's face. There was much Remo knew today that he did not understand. Having reasons for things was a Western idea. He just knew there was a gun hidden by the car door.

"You there," said the police sergeant. "What're you doing in this neighborhood?"

"Putting up a resort motel," said Remo.

"Hey, wise guy, you know where you are?"

"From time to time," said Remo cryptically.

"It's not safe here for white men."

17

Remo shrugged.

"Hey, I know you," the sergeant said. "No. It couldn't be."

He got out of the squad car, putting his revolver back in his holster.

"You know, you look like someone I used to know," said the sergeant. And Remo tried to remember the man. The sergeant's name tag read Duffy, William P., and Remo remembered a far younger man who, as a rookie, practiced quick draws with his gun. This one's face was fleshy and his eyes were tired and he smelled richly of his last meat meal. You could feel his senses were dead.

"You look almost exactly like this guy I used to know," said Sergeant Duffy. "He was raised in that orphanage. Except you're younger than he would be and you're skinnier."

"And better looking," said Remo.

"Naah, that guy was better looking. Straight as hell, that guy. Poor guy. He was a cop."

"A good cop?" asked Remo.

"Naah. Dumb, kind of. Straight, you know. They framed the poor bastard. Got the chair. Oh, more than ten years ago. Gee, you look like him."

"What do you mean he was dumb?"

"Hey, any cop what goes to the chair for doing in a pusher and then screaming that he never did it, I mean, that's stupid. There are ways to get around that sort of thing. I mean, even now when you got porkchops running the city. You just don't stand up, screaming you're innocent. If you know what I mean. The whole thing stunned the department."

"You missed him, huh?" said Remo.

"Naaah. Guy had no friends, no family, nothing.

18

It was just the idea that a cop would get it. You know. They wouldn't even let the poor bastard make a plea or nothing. You know."

"Nobody missed him," said Remo.

"Nobody. Guy was as straight as hell. A real pain in the ass."

"You still practice fast draws in the john, Duff?"

"Naah," said Duffy, then backed away, his eyes wide in horror.

"That guy's dead," he said. "Remo's dead more than ten years now. Hey. Get outta here. Get outta here or I run you in."

"What's the charge, Duff? Still confused about the correct charge?"

"No. No. This is a fucking dream," said Duffy.

"You want to see something funny, Duff? Draw," said Remo and he snapped the whole holster off the belt leaving a light brown scar on the thick black shiny leather. Sergeant Duffy's hand came down on empty space.

"You get slower as you age, meat-eater," said Remo and returned the holster-encased gun. Duffy did not see the hands move or hear the small crack of metal. Stunned, he opened his holster and parts of his revolver tinkled on the hot night sidewalk.

"Jeez. Friggin' freak," gasped Sgt. Duffy. "What'dya do with the gun? That cost me money. I'm gonna have to pay."

"We all pay, Duff."

And Duffy's partner at the wheel, hearing the commotion, came out gun drawn but found only Duffy, bewildered, staring at an empty holster ripped from his belt.

19

"He's gone," said Duffy. "I didn't even see him go and he's gone."

"Who?" said the partner.

"I didn't even see him move and now he's not here."

"Who?" said the partner.

"You remember that guy I told you about once. All the veterans knew him. Sent to the chair, no appeal, nothing. Next to the last man executed in the state. More than ten years ago, at least."

"Yeah?"

"I think I just seen him. Only he was younger and he talked funny."

Sergeant Duffy was helped back to the car and examined by the police surgeon who suggested a short rest away from a hostile urban environment. He was relieved of duty temporarily and an inspector had a long talk with his family and while he was in the Duffy household, he asked where the drill press was.

"We're looking for the power tool he used to break his gun. The police surgeon believes the gun is symbolic of his subconscious desire to leave the force," said the inspector. "Human hands don't snap a gun barrel in two."

"He didn't have no power tools," said Mrs. Duffy. "He'd just come home and drink beer. Maybe if he had a workshop, maybe he wouldn't have gone apples, huh, Inspector?"

The midday sun wilted the people on New York City's sidewalks across the Hudson from Newark. Women's spike heels sank into the soft asphalt made black gum by the heat. Remo strolled into the Plaza Hotel on Fifty-ninth Street and asked for his room key. He had been asking for his keys across the country for more than a decade now. Squirrels had nests, moles had holes, and even worms, he thought, had some piece of ground they must go to regularly. Remo had room keys. And no home.

In the elevator, a young woman in a light print purple dress that barely shielded delicate full mounds of wanting breasts commented to Remo how nice it was to be in a hotel as fine as the Plaza and wouldn't he just love to live his whole life here?

"You live in a hotel?" Remo asked.

"No. Just a split level in Jones, Georgia," said the woman, making a swift pouting face.

"It's a home," said Remo.

"It's a drag," said the woman. "I'm so excited to be here in New York City, you just don't know. Ah love it. I love it. George, he's my husband, he's here to work. But me, I'm all alone. All alone all day. I do whatever I want."

"That's nice," Remo said and watched the floor numbers blink away on the elevator panel.

"Whatever and with whoever I like," said the woman.

"That's nice," said Remo. He should have walked.

"Do you know that ninety-nine point eight percent of the women in America do not know how to make love properly?"

"That's nice."

"I'm in the point two percent that does."

"That's nice."

"Are you one of those gigolos that does it for money? You're just a doll, you know."

"That's nice," said Remo.

"I don't see anything wrong with paying for it, do you?"

21

"Paying for what?" Remo asked.

"Sex, silly."

"That's nice," said Remo and the elevator opened to his floor.

"Where you going?" said the woman. "Come back here. What's wrong?"

Remo stopped mid-hall and smiled evilly. In fact, he could not remember feeling so joyously thrilled with any idea he had entertained in the last decade. The woman blinked her soft brown eyes and said, "Wow."

"C'mere," said Remo and the woman ran to him, her breasts bobbing brightly.

"You want a thrill?"

"With you? Yeah. All right. Come on. Right on," she said.

"There's going to be a man coming down this hallway in about fifteen minutes. He's got a face like lemon juice. He'll be wearing a dark suit and a vest even in this weather. He's on the low side of sixty."

"Hey, I don't screw fossils, buddy."

"Trust me. The wildest time you've ever had. But you've got to say something special."

"What?" asked the girl suspiciously.

"You've got to say, 'Hello, Dr. Smith. I've read about you. All my friends have read about you.'"

"Who's Dr. Smith?"

"Never mind. Just tell him that and watch his face."

"Hello, Dr. Smith. Me and my friends have all read about you. Right?"

"You'll never regret it," said Remo.

"I don't know," said the woman.

Remo cupped a breast with his left hand and with

22

his right thumbed a thigh and kissed her on the neck and lips until he felt her body tremble.

"Oh, yes," she moaned. "Oh, yes. I'll say it. I— I'll say it."

"Good," said Remo and leaned her against the wall-papering of the hallway and moved five doors down where he entered.

A wisp of an Oriental in golden flowing kimono sat lotus position in front of a darkened television screen. The plush furniture of the waiting room had been moved and stacked on one side so a blue sleeping mat with its blossoms could dominate the center of the rug.

The set had been working the day before when Remo had left to look at Newark and if someone had wrecked it in between, there would be a body to be disposed of. The Master of Sinanju did not tolerate people interrupting his special television shows. Remo checked out the bathroom and the bedroom. No bodies.

"Little Father, is everything all right?"

Chiun shook his head slowly, barely moving the strand of beard.

"Nothing is right," said Chiun, the Master of Sinanju.

"Has someone broken the television?"

"Do you see the remnants of an intruder?"

"No, Chiun."

"Then how could anyone have broken my machine of dreams? No. Worse. Far, far worse."

"I'm sorry. I have a problem myself."

"You? Do you know what they have done to the beauty of the daytime dramas? Do you know the desecration that has been performed upon the life art of your nation?"

23

Remo shook his head. He didn't know. But what he gathered in the next few moments was this:

As the Planet Revolves had been irreparably ruined. Doctor Blayne Huntington had been performing a legal abortion on Janet Wofford, daughter of the shipping magnate Archibald Wofford, who was financing Dr. Huntington's experiments in nuclear transmography, when nurse Adele Richards realized the baby was probably her brother's who was serving life in Attica for leading the prison revolt against anti-feminist literature.

"Yeah?" said Remo who always had a hard time following the soap operas.

"There was physical violence," said Chiun. And as he explained it, the nurse struck the doctor. Not only was there the intrusion of violence, but she struck him wrong. It was not a blow at all.

"But they're just actors, Little Father."

"I know that now," said Chiun. "Fraud. I will not watch another show. I shall stay in America, barren of joy, without the little breezes of pleasure in a stifled old life."

Remo, his voice heavy with sadness, said that they might not be staying.

"This is a hard thing for me to tell you, Little Father," said Remo and he lowered his eyes to the carpeting, which even in the Plaza was becoming threadbare.

"The beginning of all wisdom is ignorance," said Chiun. "It is a shame that you are always at the beginning." And this thought struck the Master of Sinanju as so humorous, he repeated it and laughed. But his pupil did not laugh with him and this Chiun attributed to the famous American lack of humor.

"Perhaps you are right," said Remo. "For more

24

than a decade, I insisted I owed something to this country. For more then ten years, I've been a man without home or wealth or even a full name that is my own. I'm a man who doesn't exist. And everything I've done, I see today was useless."

"Useless?" said Chiun.

"Yes, Little Father. Useless. This country is not one bit different for my being here. It's even worse. The place where I was born is a garbage dump. The politicians are more corrupt, crime is having a full-banner field day, and—and the country is—it's coming apart."

By this, Chiun was puzzled and he said:

"You are one man, are you not?"

Remo nodded.

"There is no one emperor in this country, no one judge or priest who rules above all, is there?"

Remo nodded.

"Then, in this country with no ruler, how can you, an assassin, granted one given the sun source of all perfection in training, granted that even given the personal hand of a Master of Sinanju, masterhood yourself, a white no less, how can you feel you have failed? I do not understand this."

"You never quite understood what the organization was all about, Chiun."

"I have heard you and Smith talk. He is emperor of your organization that worships the document Constitution and you kill for its glory. This I know."

"Maybe that's how it worked out but that's not how the whole thing was planned." And Remo explained about the Constitution not working, and that it was the basic document of the country and that more than a decade before a president feared that his country would become a police state if the drift into chaos continued.

25

This, he said, Chiun must know because as keeper of the records of the House of Sinanju which had sold its services as assassins for countless centuries, he knew of many governments and he must know police states came from chaos.

"Ah," said Chiun. "You sought this chaos so that America could become like the rest of the world and you would be chief assassin of this police state. I did not understand it before."

"No," said Remo and he explained that the American Constitution was a document, a contract between all Americans with one another. And it guaranteed freedoms and rights to everyone. It was a good document. But according to its rules many evil men could operate freely. So, while keeping this contract, an American president had set up an organization which no one knew about to make sure that the country could still survive. The organization would make sure that prosecutors got proper information, dishonest judges were exposed, great organized crime families would lose their power, and all the while, the rights of the people would be protected. Doctor Harold Smith, whom Chiun called emperor, headed this organization and Remo, whom Chiun himself had trained, was the enforcement arm.

Chiun allowed that he followed Remo.

"So you see," Remo said, "there were problems. If it became known that we existed, it would be like admitting the Constitution didn't work. So secrecy was important. Well, they couldn't allow a killer arm to go around leaving fingerprints, so what they did was they got someone without a family and they removed his prints from the files in Washington by pretending he was electrocuted. Like when you first saw me, I was unconscious, right? Right?"

"When I first saw you?" said Chiun and he cackled. He did not tell Remo but white man's silliness was enough to tickle the universe. "If your fingerprints, a system of identification you think was invented in the West but was known to us thousands of years ago, if your fingerprints in these records you talk about were so important, where are your fingerprints now?"

"The fingerprints of dead people go into a special file."

"Why then did they not just put the records in the other file instead of bringing you close to death, by pretending to electrocute you?"

"Because people knew me. And they had to create a man who didn't exist for an organization that didn't exist."

"Ah," said Chiun and his long-nailed fingers formed the roofing of a Western chapel. "I see now. Of course. It is all so clear. Let us have sweet sauce for our rice. Would you like that?"

"I don't think you understand, Little Father."

"You are most clear, my son. They killed you to make you not exist so that you could work for the organization that did not exist to protect the document that does not work. All hail the wisdom of the West."

"Well, things aren't working and that's what I wanted to tell you. I've been wrong. Let us go work for the Shah of Iran or the Russians or anyone else you wish to sell our services to. I'm through with Smitty and this whole stupid thing."

"Now you confuse me," said Chiun and his voice rose to the higher pitches of joy. "You have just made a wise decision after ten years of wrong decisions and you are unhappy."

"Sure. I wasted ten years."

"Well, you have stopped wasting your life and you will never regret it. In the East, they appreciate assassins. Ah, what joyous news."

And Chiun told Remo he must allow the Master of Sinanju himself to inform Emperor Smith of the termination, because it was just as important to end services well as to begin them well, and Remo should watch closely in order that he should know the proper way to bid farewell to an emperor. For emperors did not lightly yield the cutting edge of their empires which, since history first began, had been their assassins.

When Smith knocked approximately five minutes later, the parsimonious face was in a state of frothy hysteria. The thin lips hung open like pink windsocks in a gale. The blue eyes blinked wide. He dropped his briefcase on the sleeping mat.

"Hail, Emperor Smith," said Chiun, bowing courteously.

"My god," said Smith. "My god, Remo, there's a woman outside. Our cover. It's been blown by a magazine. The whole thing's come apart. The whole thing. She read about me in a magazine. A brunette. In her twenties. Recognized me. A magazine. Our cover."

"Guess we have to close shop then, Smitty," said Remo, pulling a chair off the pile of furniture at the edge of the room and slumping down into it. His joy unplugged Smith's excitement. Smith's eyes narrowed suspiciously. He picked up his briefcase. He regained his composure.

"Did you see the young woman in the hallway?"

"As a matter of fact, Smitty, I did," said Remo.

"I see," said Smith. His voice was flat. "And after so many years and so much effort. After so many years of precise covers and broken links just to protect our security, you, for a practical joke and I assume it's that, just blabbed the whole thing to some strange biddy out in the hallway. I assume it had some deep motivation such as her breasts."

"Nope," said Remo.

"You misunderstand your loyal servant," said Chiun. "He was espousing your glory to the populace, oh wondrous emperor of CURE."

"And you explained us to Chiun also?" said Smith. "He knows what we're about."

"He extolled the glory of your Constitution. The heads of its enemies shall lie in the street. All proclaim the way of CURE," said Chiun.

"All right," said Smith. "Chiun doesn't know. What happened in the hallway? Did you go insane?"

"No. She doesn't understand any more than Chiun. She heard a name. So what? Really. Look at it. She heard a name and saw a man. Who is she? No one. And if she could make heads or tails of the whole thing, so what? So what?"

"I beg your pardon," said Smith and he looked for a place to sit.

In one slow movement, Remo was off the chair and it was sliding across the floor where it stopped just behind Smith's legs.

"I see we have tricksters. Our investment is in a juggler," said Smith. "Would you mind telling me what's happening?"

"I went home last night. Not that I have a home. I went back to that orphanage."

"You were supposed to avoid that area under any circumstances."

"The orphanage was abandoned. The whole area was abandoned. It was the center of a city and it looked like it had been bombed. And I wondered what I had been doing for the last ten years. And I wonder what you've been doing for the last ten years. The whole organization."

"I don't follow."

"We're failures. We're a waste of time. We were supposed to be this super setup to make the Constitution work. Everyone would have their freedoms while the destructive elements were put in their place. America was going through a trying time, we were supposed to help it out and then disappear with no one the wiser. We'd be here and gone. One country, one democracy saved."

"Yes?"

"What do you mean 'yes'?" said Remo. "We were a fucking waste of time. We had a president who would have been convicted of breaking and entering if he didn't get a pardon. Half the top government is in jail, the other half ought to be. You can't walk in the city streets unless you know how to kill. You read every day where this cop and that is on the take. Care for the aged has turned into a gigantic ripoff? And all this while I'm up to my armpits in bodies, supposedly ending this sort of crap."

"That's just what we're doing," said Smith.

"Hey, I'm no congressman and you're no head of a legitimate government agency. I can read newspapers, you know."

"And what you're reading, Remo, is the organization finally working. This is the pus coming out of the

30

lanced boil. Nixon wasn't the first president to do such things, he was just the first not to get away with it. His successors won't try it again. Didn't it strike you as strange that half a dozen CIA men should bungle a simple burglary? Didn't it strike you as strange that suddenly tape recordings that the former president didn't know about suddenly appear? And he can't destroy them? Remo, just how do you think we work? What you're seeing is the organization working."

Remo cocked a quizzical eyebrow. Smith continued.

"You're not seeing new crimes, Remo. You're seeing people not get away with the old ones. That nursing-home scandal goes back more than ten years. Cops on the take go back to the Revolutionary War. Cops getting sent to jail for it is new. You're seeing this country do what no other democracy has been able to do. We're cleaning house."

"Then how about the streets?"

"A little adjustment. Give us five years. Five years and the doomsayers will crawl back under their rocks. This country is coming out stronger and better."

"Why didn't I know about this?"

"Because we only use you for emergencies. You're what I use when things go wrong or can't go right any other way."

Now the Master of Sinanju had listened to this and had been quiet, for when Westerners talked silliness, no light could penetrate their shroud of ignorance. And seeing that they were now satisfied with themselves, he spoke.

"Oh, gracious Smith, how wondrous has been your success, how firm your guiding hand. Your kingdom is in order and gratefully, the House of Sinanju must take its leave, singing always the praises of Emperor Smith."

"If you wish, Chiun," said Smith. "You have trained Remo well and we are grateful, but he knows enough now to operate without you."

"There's a little problem here, Smitty," said Remo and Chiun raised his long delicate fingers, silencing Remo.

"Gracious emperor," said Chiun. "The Remo who once belonged to you now belongs to Sinanju." And seeing confusion on Smith's face, he explained that when he began training Remo, Remo had just been another American, but there was so much Sinanju training in him now that he was Sinanju, and therefore no longer Smith's but Sinanju's.

"What's he talking about?" asked Smith.

"Look," said Remo. "You give a guy a pot, right. A little dinky metal pot."

"A pale pot," added Chiun. "A miserable worthless pale pot."

"And he adds a gold handle. And a gold top. And a full inch of gold outside," said Remo.

"I like your choice of metals," said Chiun.

"Shut up," said Remo.

"Gratitude is dead," said Chiun.

"And now you've got this golden vessel with just the bare little metal left of the original pot."

"The ingratitude is what is left," said Chiun.

"Well, it's not your pot anymore," Remo told Smith.

"What are you talking about?" asked Smith.

"The mountain is not the pebble," said Chiun. "And you cannot violate this law of the universe. It is sacred."

"I'm not sure what you are getting at, Master of Sinanju, but we are willing to double in gold the payments to your village for your services. Since you regard Remo now as of Sinanju, a someday Master of Sinanju, we will pay your village for you *and* him. Double payment for double services."

"You don't understand, Smitty," said Remo.

"He most certainly does," said Chiun. "Listen to your emperor and learn of him what is your next mission."

Smith opened his briefcase. There was a problem in the Chicago grain markets that just might prove to be more disastrous for the survival of the nation than anything Remo had handled before. It had to do with the purchase of grain and famine spreading to the Western world. Even with its vast network and computers, CURE had been unable to ascertain just what was the matter. A lot of money was making peculiar things happen.

And bodies were floating up around Lake Michigan.

CHAPTER THREE

The morning sun came up over Harborcreek, Pennsylvania, as winds blew the chemical waste breezes across Lake Erie into Remo's car. Remo explained the mission to Chiun. This Chiun had demanded, since he was no longer just the trainer in the eyes of the organization. He was a coequal partner. It always amazed Remo how Chiun managed to grasp sophisticated Western concepts when it suited his purpose, like coequal partner.

This, Chiun hastened to point out, did not mean that Remo was his equal in the eyes of the universe, but only in the blurred and narrow vision of the white organization for which they worked.

"I understand, Little Father," said Remo, turning off the asphalt road into a dirty driveway. Remo could only use the sideview mirror because Chiun's lacquered wooden chests jammed full the back seat and made the rearview mirror useless unless Remo wanted to look at a pink dragon on a bright blue background.

34

"We are looking for a man named Oswald Willoughby, who is a commodities broker. He is going to testify about price-fixing on the commodities exchange. Someone or some organization dumped twenty-five million dollars worth of winter wheat on the exchange just at planting time. This caused one of the smallest plantings on record just when the world needed the most plantings. No one knows why this dumping occurred, but of the dealers who handled the bulk of the selling, two came up dead in Lake Michigan and the third is Oswald Willoughby. We're supposed to keep him alive."

Chiun thought a moment. Then he spoke.

"However," he said, "coequal does mean equal payment to Sinanju. It is good that we can get as much for quality as we can for shoddy. The villagers will appreciate my business acumen."

"You didn't understand a word I said, did you?"

"We are to keep a man alive and then you mentioned some things that could not be true."

"Like what?" snapped Remo.

"For instance, no one knows why these men were killed. This is not true. Someone knows why."

"Well, I meant we don't know."

"I could have told you of your ignorance before we left."

"You don't understand how the market works, do you? Do you?" Remo looked for a white frame cabin with a green fence. He could see steam rise from the night-cool stream flowing through the hot morning.

"You didn't understand a word about winter wheat and prices. Well, I'll tell you. If prices are high at planting time, farmers plant more grain. Most people don't buy the grain to keep. They buy it to sell. They buy it

35

now to sell at a future time, like harvesttime, when they expect the price will be more. Well, someone at planting time bought up a lot of what they call futures and dumped them on the market. Twenty-five million dollars worth. Now, while that's not much considering the total, the sudden dumping all at once sent the price skidding. Real low. It was perfect timing. Farmers couldn't get credit for large plantings and they didn't want them. So we've got a short crop this spring which explained part of the price rise in food."

"So?" said Chiun.

"So we're afraid it might get worse. That's why we've got to figure out what or who was willing to lose the bulk of twenty-five million dollars. There's a food crisis in the world."

"Why are you so worried? Sinanju has known food crises. You are telling me, you dare to tell me about food crises, you who were raised on meat and never went hungry a day in your life."

"Oh, Jeez," moaned Remo for he knew he would now hear the story of Sinanju, how because of starvation the village of Sinanju had to put their newly born babies into the cold waters of the West Korea Bay, how the village was food-poor, and how the Masters of Sinanju were born in desperation, how each Master for centuries had rented his services as an assassin to emperors and kings in far-off lands so that never again would the villagers have to send the babies "back to sleep" in the waters of the bay.

"Never again," said Chiun.

"It's more than fifteen hundred years since that happened," said Remo.

"When we say never again, we mean never again,"

36

said Chiun. "This is your tradition now also. You should learn it."

It sounded like a pot banging a pot down the road, through the scrub pines, whipped short with almost greenless branches by the Lake Erie winds. It sounded dull in the morning air that made the car seat sticky. It sounded like a little pop that morning sleepers shouldn't notice. It was a shot.

Remo saw a dark man run from the white house with the green fence. He tucked something into his belt as he trotted to a waiting pink Eldorado with its motor running. The car took off before the door was shut, a fast but not screeching start, kicking up little dust flurries. The driver intended to pass Remo on the left as all oncoming cars should. Remo occupied the lane. Chiun, who thought seat belts were bondage and was not about to wear one, caught the car crash with a slight upward motion lifting his light frame so that at the moment of impact, he was aloft. Two long fingernails of the right hand caught the dashboard in such a way that it looked as if he were doing a mild vertical one-handed pushup. The other hand caught flying glass. Remo stopped his forward motion with an elbow against the wheel and the same free flight uplift as the Master.

The door popped open and he was out of the car, on the road before the cars stopped their first spin. He caught the Eldorado, snapping open a door, and reached in past a bloody body to put on the brake.

He dragged the two still forms from the Eldorado and saw that the dark man had a gun in his belt. It smelled of a fresh shot. Remo felt for a heartbeat. It was the last strong flutter of a muscle about to die. It stopped.

The driver's heart was better. Remo felt around the body. Only a shoulder bone had that squishy loose feeling of a break. The face flowed red from glass cuts but it was not serious. Remo maneuvered his hand underneath the man's jaw, working on veins going up through the neck. The man's eyelids opened.

"Ooooh," he groaned. "Ooooooh."

"Hi there," said Remo.

"Ooooooh," groaned the man. He was in his late forties and his face was a remnant of a teenage battle with acne. The acne had won.

"You're going to die," said Remo.

"Oh, my God, no. No."

"Your partner made the hit on Willoughby, didn't he? Oswald Willoughby."

"Was that the guy's name?"

"Yes. Who sent you?"

"Get me a doctor."

"It's too late. Don't go with this sin on your soul," said Remo.

"I don't want to die."

"You want to go without a confession? Who sent you?"

"No one special. It was just a hit. A five-grand hit. It was supposed to be easy."

"Where'd you get the money?"

"Joe got it. At Pete's."

"Where's Pete's?"

"East St. Louis. I was needing. I needed the dough. I was just out of Joliet. Couldn't get work."

"Where's Pete's?"

"Off Ducal Street."

"That's a great help."

"Everybody knows Pete's."

"Who gave you the money for the hit?"

"Pete."

"You're a great help. Just Pete at Pete's in East St. Louis."

"Yeah. Get me a priest. Please. Someone. Anyone."

"Just rest here," said Remo.

"I'm dying. Dying. My shoulder's killing me."

Remo checked out the small white house. The door was shut but unlocked. The killer had had the presence of mind not to leave it ajar so that the body would probably not have been found until it made a stink.

Willoughby probably got it in bed, thought Remo, as he entered the house. But then he saw the TV lit with the sound turned low, and a silent interviewer asking a silent question to elicit a silent response, and Remo knew Willoughby had spent the night here in the living room. His last night.

The room smelled of stale whiskey. Willoughby lay on a couch behind the door, an open bottle of Seagram's Seven and an unfinished Milky Way on a tarnished end table. Willoughby's brains were spread out on the high back of the couch, powder burns on the close temple. A phone rang. It was under the couch. Remo answered it.

"Yeah," he said, lifting the phone and resting the base on Willoughby's stomach.

"Oh, hello, darling." It was a woman's voice. "I know I'm not supposed to phone but the garbage disposal is stuck. It's been stuck since dinner, Ozzie. I know I'm not supposed to call. Should I get the repairman? I'll get the repairman. It's the cauliflower that does it. And we don't even like cauliflower. You like it. I don't know why cauliflower. I don't even know why they told you not to give me the number. I mean, who have these few phone calls I've made hurt? Right? Who have they hurt? Ozzie . . . are you there?"

Remo tried to answer but the only suitable answers were lies and he pressed down the receiver button terminating the conversation. He left the phone off the cradle, buzzing a useless dial tone.

What was he going to tell her? That her phone calls had ruined Willoughby's only protection, the secrecy of his whereabouts? She had enough grief coming. By the time the dial tone turned into a continuous out-of-order whine, Remo found a stack of notes in the kitchen. They were in an old Eaton Corrasable Bond Box and there was a title page: "Testimony of Oswald Willoughby."

Remo took the box. Outside, the driver of the hit car was discovering that he only had a broken bone. He leaned against the fender of the smashed-up car, pressing tight his injured shoulder with his free hand.

"Hey, I'm not gonna die. You're a damned liar, fella, a damned liar."

"No, I'm not," said Remo and with an ease of motion that made his right hand seem hardly to move at all, he let his index and forefinger out, penetrating the skull, which jerked the man's head back as if it had met a crane-hoisted wrecking ball. The feet flew over the head and the man slapped into the dust, silently and finally, without even a twitch of the spine.

Chiun, noticing that even to the breathing the blow had been without flaw, turned back to his trunks. They were undamaged. But they might have been and he told his pupil that such carelessness as his car driving could not be tolerated.

"We've got to get out of here and your trunks are

40

slowing us down, Little Father. Maybe I'd better do this assignment alone," Remo said.

"We are coequal. I am not only your superior in training but on assignments now, by order of Emperor Smith I am on the same level. My judgment is of equal weight to yours. My responsibility is equal to yours. Therefore you cannot say anymore, go home, Master of Sinanju, I will do this or do that alone. It is *we*. *We* do this or *we* do not do that. It is *we*. Never *you* anymore, but *we*. No more *yous*. *We*."

"Willoughby, the man we're supposed to keep alive, is dead," said Remo.

"You failed," said Chiun.

"But there's some crucial evidence in this box," said Remo.

"We have saved the evidence. Good."

"It's not as good as Willoughby himself."

"You aren't perfect."

"But for the first time though, there's a lead on the source which just might be the core of the whole thing."

"We have the solution."

"Possibly," said Remo.

"Fate takes strange patterns at times," said Chiun. "We may succeed gloriously, as is the tradition of the House of Sinanju, or you may fail, which would not be the first time in your life."

In the matter of the trunks, Chiun explained that they had to take them along because their mission was to honor the Constitution of the United States and to wear one kimono continuously would be to dishonor the document by which Remo's nation lived. Chiun understood these things now, being coequal.

The driver of a pickup truck understood the need to get the trunks to the closest airport immediately and

41

to forget about the wrecked cars and the two dead bodies he saw when his country's history was shown to him. Fifteen portraits of Ulysses S. Grant, printed in green.

"You fellas want a lift, well, I'll show you, the spirit of cooperation is not dead. That's fifteen of them little fellers. Thirteen . . . fourteen . . . and fifteen."

The Piper they rented circled over the Mississippi River town of East St. Louis because Chiun wanted to see it from the air.

"That is a fine river," said Chiun. "Who owns the water rights?"

"No one exactly owns the water rights. It belongs to the country."

"Then the country could give it to us in payment?"

"No," said Remo.

"Even if we glorify the Constitution?"

"Not even then."

"You were born in an ungrateful country," said Chiun, but Remo did not answer him. He was thinking about Willoughby's testimony. Willoughby did not give his life for it. He gave his life because he let his wife know where he was. People died, not for causes, but for stupidity or bad luck, which was another form of stupidity, caused by incompetence. This was the essence of what he had been taught for more than a decade. In the world there was competence and incompetence and nothing else. Causes were frills and came and went with each age. Luck was only the cloudy explanation for things people did not perceive. In this, the Master of Sinanju, more than fourscore in years, stood alone, atop the world.

A man like Willoughby had worked his entire life without knowing what he did. He took orders and he executed orders and nowhere in his testimony did it ever show that he understood more than a minimum about how food was grown and gotten to market. He had laced the testimony he had hoped to give with words like "hard futures" and "soft futures" and the market strengthening. Remo knew in his stomach that this was not how his country had become the greatest food producer in the world.

There was talk today about his country being selfishly food-rich, but all those talking like that made it seem as if the food just grew by itself because the land was rich. This was not so. Men planted seed, and sweated over seed, and tried to outsmart the weather. Men invested their lives in the soil, from the laboratories where Americans sought constantly improving grains and fertilizers, to the iron shops of Detroit where men improved the substitute for the ox, the tractor. America had invented the automatic reapers. America had made the first real changes in agriculture since man had left the caves and put seed in soil. America's food wealth was the fruit of its character. Genius, hard work, and persistence.

It deeply offended Remo when he heard it compared to coal or oil or bauxite, generally by some man in a university who had never broken sweat on his brow.

What made a country developed or underdeveloped was its people. Yet these men who knew not of labor referred to the natural resources of undeveloped countries as something belonging, by some divine right, solely to the people who happened to live over them, while at the same time they said the proceeds of those who worked for food belonged to the whole world. If it were not for the real workers of the world, the oil and bauxite and copper lying under sand and jungle would be as useless to the underdeveloped nations as they had been at the first tick of noticed time.

As Chiun had so well taught, there was only competence and incompetence.

Willoughby happened to be one of the ones taking a free ride. Nearly one hundred pages of written testimony and the man only suspected that he was stumbling onto the greatest man-made disaster in history.

"I don't know how," concluded Willoughby's written statement, "but these peculiar investment patterns forebode, I believe, a master plan of destruction. The depression of the winter wheat market futures at planting appear computer-timed to highest impact for maximum potential in minimizing food growth." Whatever the neon wool that all meant. All the testimony lacked was advice to get into this wonderful thing with your money while the getting was good.

Willoughby had made eighty thousand dollars a year as a commodities analyst, according to Smith's information.

In East St. Louis, you could see the heat rising from the cracked sidewalks of Ducal Street, a row of two-story wooden buildings and storefronts, most of them empty. Pete's Pool Parlour had its windows painted green halfway up. It wasn't empty. A very large red-blotched face with shiny grease and rheumy black eyes stared over the green paint line. The garbage pail of a face rested dully under an immaculate bright red hat with pompon. Inside, Remo and Chiun saw it had a body, large hairy arms like girders with fur transplants hanging out of a worn leather vest. The hands ended at the denim-covered groin where they occupied themselves with scratching.

"Where's Pete?" asked Remo.

The face did not answer.

"I'm looking for Pete."

"Who are you and dinko?" said the garbage pail of a face.

"I'm the spirit of Christmas Past and this is Mother Goose," said Remo.

"You got a big mouth."

"It's a hot day. Tell me where Pete is, please," said Remo. Chiun examined the strange room. There were green rectangular tables with colored balls. The white ball did not have a number. There were sticks with which young men pushed the white ball into other balls. When certain of these other balls went into holes at the sides of the table, the man hitting the white ball into the colored balls was allowed to continue or, in some cases, collected paper money, which, while not gold, could be used to purchase things. Chiun went over to the table where the most money was changing hands.

Meanwhile, Remo finished his business.

"Just tell me where Pete is."

The hairy hand left the groin to rub thumb against forefinger, indicating money.

"Give me something," said the garbage pail of a face. So Remo gave him a shattered collarbone and, true to his word, the garbage pail of a face told him that Pete was behind the cash register and then he passed out from the pain. Remo nudged the man's face with his shoe. There was a grease spot on the floor.

Pete was holding a weapon behind the cash register when Remo got there.

"Hi, I'd like to speak to you privately," said Remo.

"I saw what you did there. Just stay where you are."

Remo's right hand fluttered with his fingers almost

45

braiding themselves. Pete's eyes followed the hand for a fraction of an instant. Which they were supposed to do. In that moment, just as the eyes moved, Remo's left hand was behind the counter in simultaneous flow, thumb into metacarpals, pressuring the nerves into a gel of compressed bone. The gun dropped on a box of pool chalk. Pete's eyes teared. A crazy pain-racked smile came across his otherwise bland face.

"Wow, that smarts," Pete said.

A lounger whiling away his twenties and thirties would have seen only the thin man with the thick wrists go over to Pete and walk with him to a back room, holding Pete's arm in some sort of friendly embrace. A lounger, however, would have been more interested in the strange elderly Oriental with the funny robes.

Waco Boy Childers was playing Charlie Dusset for a hundred dollars a game and no one was talking, excepting that funny Oriental fella. He wanted to know the rules of the game.

Waco Boy lowered his stick and sighed.

"Pops, I was shooting," said Waco Boy down to the old squint of a gook. "People do not talk while I am shooting."

"Do you perform so well that it robs others of breath?" asked Chiun.

"Sometimes. If they got enough money on it."

This brought laughs.

"Like, watch Charlie Dusset," said Waco Boy. Chiun cackled and both Waco Boy and Charlie asked what he was laughing about.

"Funny names. Your names are so funny. 'Dusset.' 'Waco Boy.' You have such funny names," and Chiun's laughter was infectious for those crowding around the

46

table laughed also, except Waco Boy and Charlie Dusset.

"Yeah? What's your name, feller?" said Waco Boy.

And Chiun told them his name, but in Korean. They did not understand.

"I think that's funny," said Waco Boy.

"Fools usually do," said Chiun and this time even Charlie Dusset laughed.

"You want to put your money where your mouth is?" said Waco Boy. He set his hand bridge on the green felt top and with a smooth-honed stroke put away the seven ball in the side pocket, the eight ball on a bank the length of the table, which left the cue ball right behind the nine at a corner pocket. He put the yellow nine away with a short stroke that left the cue ball dead where it hit. Charlie Dusset paid out with his last bill.

"I presume you wish me to gamble?" said Chiun.

"You presumes correctly."

"On the outcome of this game?"

"Correct," said Waco Boy.

"I do not gamble," said Chiun. "Gambling makes a person weak. It robs him of his self-worth, for a man who places his fate in luck instead of in his own skills surrenders his well-being to the whims of fortune."

"You're just a talker then?"

"I did not say that."

Waco Boy grabbed a roll of bills out of his pockets and threw them on the green felt table. "Put up or shut up."

"Do you have gold?" said Chiun.

"I thought you didn't gamble," said Waco Boy.

"Defeating you in any contest of skill is not gambling," said Chiun and this remark almost leveled Charlie Dusset with laughter.

"I got a gold watch," said Waco Boy and before he could get it off his wrist, the long fingernails of the Oriental had it off and then back on while Waco Boy's stubby fingers seemed to grub hopelessly.

"It is not gold," said Chiun. "But since I have nothing else to do at this moment, I shall play you for that paper. This is gold."

From his kimono, Chiun took out a large thick coin, shiny and yellow. And he put it on the edge of the table. But the people around allowed they didn't know if it were real gold.

"It is an English Victoria, accepted the whole world over."

And the folks around the table allowed it sure was a fine-looking coin and someone said he had read about British Victorias and they were sure worth a lot of money. But Waco Boy said as he didn't quite know if he wanted to risk $758 against a single coin, no matter how much it was worth.

Chiun added another coin.

"Or even two," said Waco Boy. "Maybe a hundred against one of them."

"I will offer two against your paper of what you think is a hundred valuation."

"Better watch out, Mister," said Charlie Dusset. "Waco Boy's the best in the whole state. All Missouri."

"All of Missouri?" said Chiun, clasping a long delicate hand to his chest. "Next you will tell me he is the best in all America and then the continent."

"He's pretty good, Mister," said Charlie Dusset. "He cleaned me out."

"Ah, what formidableness. Nevertheless, I will take my poor chances."

"You want to break?" asked Waco Boy.

"What is break?"

"Taking the first shot."

"I see. And how is this game won? What are the rules?"

"You take this cue stick and you hit the white ball into first the one ball and you knock that in. Then the two and so on until the nine. When you get the nine you win."

"I see," said Chiun. "And what if the nine should go in on the first stroke?"

"You win."

"I see," said Chiun as Waco Boy placed the nine balls in a diamond formation at the other end of the table. And Chiun asked to hold the balls to see what they felt like and Waco Boy rolled him one and he lifted it and asked to see another, but Waco Boy said they were all identical. To this, Chiun answered no, they were not all identical. The blue one was not as perfectly round as the orange one and the green one was heavier than all the rest and although those around him laughed, Chiun persisted in feeling every one of the balls, and had they noticed that when he rolled them back they stopped on the table exactly where they had been in the rack, they might have expected what would happen next.

Chiun had but one question before he took a short cue stick.

"Yeah, what is it?" said Waco Boy.

"Which is the nine ball?"

"The yellow one."

"There are two yellow ones."

"The striped one with the nine on it."

"Oh, yes," said Chiun, for the nine had been on the underside of the ball.

Those around would later say the old Oriental man had held the cue stick in a peculiar way. Sort of one hand in the middle, kind of. No bridge. Like a nail file almost. Alls he did was like flick it. Just flick and that cue ball'd got wham-bam spinnin' like you never seen. Drove right into the center of the rack and like zap. Clipped that nine and smacked it dead into the left corner pocket.

"Jeeezus," said Waco Boy.

"No. Not him," said Chiun. "Arrange the balls again."

And this time, because the rack was pressed with more tightness than the first, Chiun sent the white ball first into the rack to release the nine, so that the white ball coming off the left cushion caught it properly and propelled it into the right corner pocket.

In such a manner, he won seven games with seven strokes and all around wished to know who he was.

"You have heard in your lifetimes that no matter how good you are, there is always someone better?" said Chiun.

Everyone allowed as how they had heard that.

"I am that person. The someone better."

Remo, meanwhile, attended to business. In a forthright manner, he asked Pete simply why he had promised five thousand dollars to two men to kill Oswald Willoughby. Pete answered forthrightly. He had gotten ten thousand for it and paid out five. The money had come from Johnny "Deuce" Deussio who had proprietary interests in numbers, gambling, and narcotics in East St. Louis. Deussio, it was said, worked for

50

Guglielmo Balunta, who had a proprietary interest in all St. Louis. Pete noted he would be killed for saying this about Johnny Deuce. Of course, Deussio might be too late. Pete also noted that it would be nice if Remo could possibly return his intestines to his body cavity.

"They're not gone. It only feels like that. Nerves."

"That's nice," said Pete. "It's good to know it only feels like my stomach's been ripped out."

Remo worked the muscles near Pete's ribs taking pressure off the intestinal tract.

"Oh, my god, that feels good," said Pete. "Thank you. It feels like my stomach is back in."

"You won't tell anyone I've been here, will you?" asked Remo.

"Are you kidding? Mess with you?"

John Vincent Deussio, president of Deussio Realty and Deussio Enterprises Inc., had a steel-link fence around his estate just outside St. Louis. He had electronic eyes near the fence and what might charitably be described as a herd of Doberman Pinschers. He had twenty-eight bodyguards under command of his *capo regime* who was his cousin, Salvatore Mangano, one of the most feared men west of the Mississippi.

So what was he doing in his alabaster-tiled bathroom about three A.M. with his face in the flushing toilet? He knew it was about three A.M. because on an uplift which felt like his hair was coming out of his head, he saw his watch and one of the hands, which was probably the hour hand, was pointing toward his fingers. What was he doing? He was waking up. That was first. Secondly, he was answering questions which came rapidly now. He liked to answer those questions. When he did so, he could breathe and John Vincent Deussio had liked to breathe ever since he was a little baby.

51

"I got fifty grand from a friend of mine in a coast public relations agency. Feldman, O'Connor and Jordan. They're big. I was doing a favor. They wanted this guy Willoughby. I've done a lot of work for them lately."

"Commodities people?" came the next question. It was a man's voice. He had thick wrists. He was flushing the toilet again.

"Yes. Yes. Yes. Commodities."

"Who gave you the contracts?"

"Giordano. Giordano. That's Jordan's real name. It's a big agency. They got some kind of wonder grain. Gonna save the world. Make a fucking fortune."

"And what about Balunta?"

"He's gonna get his cut. I wasn't gonna hold out on him. For a crummy fifty grand. He didn't have to ask like this."

"So Balunta didn't have anything to do with this?"

"He's gonna get his cut. He's gonna get it. What is this shit?" And John Vincent Deussio saw the toilet flush again and everything became dark and when he awoke it was four A.M. and he was retching. He yelled for his cousin, Sally. Sally hadn't seen anyone, maybe Johnny Deuce had dreamed it, sort of sleepwalking like. No one had gotten in during the night. They checked the fences and checked the men who handled the dogs and checked the bodyguards and even called in this Japanese guy they had hired once as a consultant. He smelled the ground.

"Impossible," he said. "I gave you my word that even the greats of Ninja, the night-fighters of the Orient, could not penetrate your castle and I stand by my word. Impossible."

"Maybe somebody better than Ninja?" asked Johnny

Deuce, who was now getting quizzical looks from his cousin Sally.

"Ninja is the best," said the Japanese.

"Maybe you dreamed it, like I said," said Sally.

"Shut up, Sally. I didn't dream my head into a fucking toilet bowl." And turning to the consultant, he asked again if he was sure that there was nothing better than Ninja.

"In the world today, no," said the muscular Japanese. "In the martial arts, one art breeds another art and thus today there are many. But it is said, and I believe, that they all came from one, the sun source of the arts it is called. And the farther from the source, the less potent. The closer, the more potent. We are almost direct from this source. We are Ninja."

"What's the source?"

"Some claim but I do not believe that they have even met him."

"Who?"

"The Master. The Master of Sinanju."

"A yellow guy?"

"Yes."

"I saw a wrist. It was white."

"Impossible then. No one outside this small Korean town has ever possessed Sinanju." He smiled. "Let alone a white person. But it is only legend."

"I told you you was dreaming," said Sally, who didn't quite know why he got a slap in the face just then.

"I know I wasn't dreaming," said Deussio, as he phoned his contact on the coast and, in veiled words because you always had to assume someone was tapping your line, told Mr. Jordan that something had gone wrong with the recent account operations.

CHAPTER FOUR

"What went wrong?" asked James Orayo Fielding from his Denver offices. He glanced at his two-faced digital calendar clock. The inside figure read three months, eighteen days. He had stopped looking at the outside figure when the fainting spells had started two weeks and five days before.

"I don't have time for anything to go wrong," he said into the telephone receiver. The office was air-conditioned yet he was sweating.

"Are the fields all right? Someone's gotten to the fields. I know it."

"I don't think that's it," came the voice of William Jordan, vice president of Feldman, O'Connor and Jordan. "In the overview, you're still in a highly positive launch position."

"I know what that means. You haven't done anything yet. Is the Mojave Field all right? That's the most important one."

"Yes. As far as I know," said Mr. Jordan.

54

"Is the field in Bangor, Maine, all right?"

"Bangor is top-notch."

"The Sierra field? There can be mountain floods, you know."

"Sierra is high."

"And Piqua, Ohio?"

"Buckeye beautiful."

"So what could have gone wrong?" Fielding demanded.

"I can't talk about it on the phone, Mr. Fielding. It's in that sensitive area."

"Well, get over here and tell me."

"You couldn't come here, sir? I'm rather chockablock with work."

"Do you want to keep this account?" said Fielding.

"I can wedge in time this afternoon."

"You bet you can," said Fielding. "If you want to make millions."

He hung up the receiver and felt better. He had Feldman, O'Connor and Jordan just where he wanted them, just under his heel. If he had paid them a fancy retainer, they would have given him fancy footwork. But he had hung a piece of sweet bait just out of reach of their quivering tentacles, and that kept them scurrying where he wanted them to scurry. They smelled a monumental fortune and they had already killed for it.

Fielding swiveled his chair to face the large picture window filled by the Rockies, the new playground of the mindless. The Rockies had killed men since the Indians came down across the Bering Strait. Froze them like flies in the winter, let them thaw out and stink in the summer. White men came, built their little protected nests, briefly stuck their fur-wrapped faces into the air, and said how beautiful nature was. Beautiful? Nature killed.

Fielding looked at the Rockies and remembered the first meeting with Feldman, O'Connor, and Jordan nearly eight months before. Everything had been so Christmassy in December. The commodities market had taken that dip and there was less winter wheat growing under the snows of America's plains than at any time since the Thirties.

Feldman and O'Connor and Jordan had greeted him personally for their presentation. Lights of red and green and blue hung from palm trees. A ceramic Santa Claus which dispensed scotch from its groin leaned against a bookcase. Feldman nervously explained it was left over from the office Christmas party. He had a smooth tan with manicured gray hair and a pinky ring with a diamond big enough to send sun signals half way across the country. O'Connor was pale with freckles and large bony hands that worked themselves together. His blue striped tie was knotted tight enough for a penance. And then there was Jordan, even-capped white teeth, black hair so neatly billowing it looked as if it had come from a cheap plastic mold. Eyes like black immies. He wore a dark striped suit with too-wide shoulders and too-flaring lapels and, of all things, a buckle in the back. The buckle was silver.

Fielding entered the room like a modest lord among gaudy servants.

"It is truly an honor to have you here, sir," said Feldman. "And I might add, a pleasure."

"A real pleasure," said O'Connor.

"A deep pleasure," said Jordan.

"There is no pleasure for me, gentlemen," said Fielding as Feldman took his coat and O'Connor his briefcase. "I am in mourning for a beautiful person. You may never have heard of him. No history books will carry his name to future generations, no songs will praise his deeds. Yet truly this person was a man among men."

"I'm sorry to hear that," Feldman had said.

"The good die young," said O'Connor.

"Most distressing," said Jordan.

"His name was Oliver. He was my manservant," said Fielding.

"A good manservant is better than a rotten scientist," Feldman had allowed. O'Connor thought so too.

"A good manservant is the closest thing to Christ on earth," said Jordan. Feldman had to agree with that. O'Connor noted that in his faith it was the highest honor to be called handmaiden of the Lord.

"I am determined that his name will be remembered. I am determined that men will say Oliver with respect, reverence, and yes, even joy. That is why I am here."

"We can set it to music," said Feldman and he began to hum a Negro spiritual and then created the words to the music. "Anybody here see my old friend, Oliver?"

Fielding shook his head. "No," he said.

"You're not focusing for prime thrust," said Jordan to Feldman.

"Not at all," said O'Connor.

"I have a better idea," said Fielding.

"I like it," said Feldman.

"I have set up a foundation with an original endowment of my entire fortune, fifty million dollars."

"Beautiful," said Feldman.

"Solid," said O'Connor.

"Beautifully solid base," said Jordan.

"It's more than a base, gentlemen," said Fielding and

he signaled for his briefcase. "As you gentlemen know, I have been involved in industry, successfully involved, except for a few minor tax losses in the southwest."

"And a leader of the Denver community," said Feldman.

"A solid leader," said O'Connor. "As were your parents and grandparents."

"The sort of client we would be proud to represent," said Jordan.

Fielding opened the briefcase. Carefully he took from it four plastic boxes with metal latches. The boxes were clear plastic and contained grain of white and brown and golden colors. One was labeled "soybean," another "wheat," another "rice," and another "barley."

"These are the basic grains of man's sustenance," said Fielding.

"They have a natural beauty," said Jordan.

"I feel better since I've started eating granola," said Feldman.

"The staff of life," said O'Connor.

"First I have a small request. Please refrain from comments until I ask for them," said Fielding. "You are looking at four miracles. You are looking at the answer, the final answer to man's problems with famine. These grains were grown in a single month's time."

There was silence in the room. Fielding paused. When he saw the three partners' eyes start to wander uncomfortably, he went on.

"I don't think you are aware of what a month-grown grain is. It is more than a faster process. It's twelve crops a year where a farmer had only one or two before. Through my process, we can increase the food yield a minimum of six times on earth. In all weather and in all conditions. I need only one thing now. A demonstration, well-publicized, to commit the world—especially the underdeveloped world—to this process. It is important, vitally important now, because I hear the winter wheat crop this year will be a small one."

"Who owns the patent?" asked O'Connor.

"It is not patented. It is a secret process I intend to give to all mankind," said Fielding.

"But for your protection, don't you think it would be wise to have some sort of patent? We could arrange it."

Fielding shook his head. "No. But what I will do for your services is give your firm 20 percent of the profit on every soybean, every grain of rice, grain of wheat, or barley grown in the world."

O'Connor's tie knot bobbed, Feldman salivated, and Jordan, his eyes glowing, breathed heavily.

"The entire world is going to use what I call the Oliver method, in tribute to my noble servant."

The three men bowed their heads and Fielding passed out pictures of Oliver, taken by a sheriff's office after the air accident. He said he would appreciate it if they would keep those pictures in their offices. They agreed. But it was when they saw the demonstration that they vowed ultimate fidelity to the memory of Oliver.

In Rocky Mountain winter, they saw a twenty-yard patch of snowy mountainside planted with wheat treated by the Oliver method, as Fielding had called it. Saw workmen pickax into the soil and cover the seed with rock-hard pieces of ground and returned thirty days later to see stalks of wheat growing in the sub-zero wind.

"The weather is only a slight hindrance to the Oliver method," Fielding yelled above the wind. O'Connor pocketed a stalk with his gloved hand. Back in Los Angeles, they got the verdict from a biologist.

"Yep. This is wheat all right."

Could it have been grown on a mountainside in winter?"

"No way."

If it could be, grown full in just one month, what would you say?

"Whoever knew how to do it would be the richest man in the world."

That report from the biologist had come seven months before. Fielding had waited two days for them to get the biologist's report, as he knew they would, and then he had brought his little problem to Jordan. In an effort to make the market more receptive to fast-grown grains, Fielding had sold winter wheat futures massively with funds from the Oliver Foundation. He was troubled by this. A couple of commodities brokers suspected something. Some were trying to blackmail him. A third might be considering telling the government. There was nothing else to do but confess all and give the formula for Wondergrains—Feldman, O'Connor and Jordan had changed what they called the packaging concept from the Oliver method to Wondergrains—to the public. Just announce it and give it away. Free.

"Don't worry. I'll take care of everything, Mr. Fielding. Just you protect our little project, eh?" said Jordan, which was what Fielding knew he would say, which was why he had selected Feldman, O'Connor and Jordan, whom he knew to be Giordano with many cousins who could make people disappear.

And there were a few more people who had threatened to get in the way, people who had intruded upon the orderly plan to bring Wondergrains to the world.

And Fielding had presented their names to Jordan in a kind of laundry list for mass murder, and Jordan had said he would take care of everything.

It had worked so well, thought Fielding. He had combined his public relations element with his killer-arm element and with luck, he would live to see the fruits of his project—the vast and utter destruction of entire civilizations. Without luck, it would happen anyway. It was too late to stop it.

His digital desk calendar predicted he had three months, eighteen days to live. The project itself should be finalized in a little more than a month.

The intercom intruded upon his reverie. It was his new secretary. He always had new secretaries. They didn't stay more than a week.

"I have the list for tomorrow's demonstration," came her wriggly voice.

"Bring it in."

"Could I slip it under the door?"

"Of course not."

"Those pictures in your office. They're sort of . . . sort of stomach-turning."

"Those pictures," said Fielding looking at the sheriff's impact shots of Oliver, "are what this whole foundation is about. When I hired you, I asked if you were committed to decency and you said yes. Well, I'm not going to put up lying pictures around the office. He died horribly and I want the world to know that. I want them to know the truth about Oliver. The truth will set you free."

She brought in the lists with her eyes fixed on the mauve carpeting. She did not even look up when she handed Fielding the lists. Pakistan had officials at the Sierra and Mojave for the first planting. Chad, Senegal,

61

and Mali were listed for the Mojave as those countries afflicted by drought opted mainly for the desert demonstrations. Russia and China were scheduled for desert, mountain, midwest, and north. England was scheduled for Bangor, Maine, and France for Ohio.

But nowhere on the lists was India.

"Did you phone the Indian Embassy?" asked Fielding.

"Yes sir."

"Why aren't they coming? We've spent close to $700,000 on pamphlets, brochures, charts, photos. Feldman, O'Connor and Jordan had a postage bill of over $20,000. I know India was informed."

"Well, they said they didn't have anyone available."

"They have four agricultural experts in the United States. I know that for a fact. I know their names. India is the most important country on that list."

"Yes sir, I know that. Please don't yell. I have it written down outside."

Fielding watched her scurry from the office. The intercom buzzed on.

"Sir, the four agricultural experts assigned to the Indian embassy are occupied tomorrow as follows: one is lecturing at Yale on America's responsibility to share its food; another is a panel member on . . . I have the title right here . . . 'America the Monster' . . . he said he would have liked to come to the demonstration but the ambassador made him go to the panel discussion on the threat of being sent back to India if he didn't. The third is speaking on American hypocrisy at Berkeley . . . he never goes to any agricultural exhibits anyhow . . . and the fourth is sick with stomach cramps. Too much rich American food or something."

"But they must know this is the miracle grain."

"Their only answer, sir, was that they're too busy fighting hypocrisy. Perhaps if we told them the process was part of a nuclear weapon. When I mentioned nuclear, they were very interested until they found out it only had to do with the seeds."

"No," said Fielding.

When Jordan arrived that afternoon to discuss his little problem, Fielding demanded that an Indian representative be at one demonstration at least.

"It's critical. India is the most important market of all," said Fielding.

"India doesn't buy foodstuffs. I've checked this out thoroughly," said Jordan. "If you give them grains on credit, they take them, because if they wait long enough the credit will be forgotten. But their policy, and it has generally worked, Mr. Fielding, is that if there's a surplus of grain anywhere, they're going to get it free anyhow. They'd rather put their money in nuclear devices."

"But they have an incredible famine problem. I've seen it myself."

"Mr. Fielding, do you remember what India did last year? First they announced that they were not going to accept any more grain from the United States which had given them something like $16 billion— that's billion—in free food. Then, to punish the imperialist American monsters, they supported the Arab oil squeeze. When oil prices went up, so did the price of fertilizer. It tripled. India couldn't buy any, because all their money was going into nuclear bombs. So they asked America for more free food. And we gave it to them."

"That's insane."

"So's India," said Jordan. "If we paid them to take

the Wondergrain, they'd take it. But they're not going to buy it."

"Then we'll have to arrange some kind of credit for them," said Fielding, "or else India will become . . . ." And he did not finish his sentence for it would have disclosed that if India did not buy the Wondergrain, it would become the food-richest nation on earth. What was left of earth.

"All right. What's the problem you mentioned?" said Fielding.

Fortunately, it turned out to be minor. It had taken months for Jordan's people to locate that talky commodities man, that Willoughby. One of the men who had arranged Willoughby's "accident" had had his house invaded. Mr. Fielding should be careful for the next few weeks. Check his door locks and things like that.

"This was the only slipup," Jordan said. "The other commodities people, those other names you gave me, all of them were handled. Just this little problem and I think you should be careful."

"I've been careful all my life. It's too late to be careful now," said Fielding. And he warned Jordan that if India were not part of the Wondergrain plan, Feldman, O'Connor and Jordan might find itself without its percentage.

Of course, thought Fielding without mentioning it, if India became the most workable nation on earth, that would be almost as good as eliminating all the bugs all together.

CHAPTER FIVE

Remo and Chiun saw the demonstration site down the flat highway. A herd of limousines, television trucks, and police vehicles surrounded a high fence on a rise three miles off, baking in the summer desert.

"I do not believe food could grow here," said Chiun and once again told the story of how poor soil had forced Sinanju to send its best sons to foreign lands to earn food for the village. The way Chiun told it, a callow youth had ventured forth into a hostile world with nothing but his hands, his mind, and his character.

"You were forty when you became Master of Sinanju," said Remo.

"Fifty or a hundred, a new experience makes children of us all," said Chiun.

In his search for Jordan who had paid Johnny Deussio who had paid Pete who paid the two who died in Harborcreek after killing Willoughby, Remo had been told by an all-too-bubbly secretary that Mr. Jordan "will be at the most major agricultural advancement since the plow."

"Where?" Remo had asked.

"The stunning great step of mankind by the one small agricultural step of one man, James Orayo Fielding."

"Where?"

"The salvation of the world which is what you might call this Wondergrain. For . . . ."

"Just tell me where it's happening," and hearing "the Mojave Desert," Remo asked where in the Mojave and endured another three minutes of windy wonder until he got the exact location. That was yesterday. They rented a car and drove and there were Chiun's trunks right in the back seat and in the car trunk.

"I feel like a porter," Remo had said, loading the large colorful trunks into the car. "Could you make it on one less trunk, maybe?"

To this question, Chiun had had a sudden attack of only being able to speak Korean, and since Remo had picked up some Korean over the years, Chiun could speak only a Pyongyang dialect which Remo did not know.

As they neared the demonstration site, Chiun's English naturally improved, especially when he found an excuse to repeat the legend of Sinanju. He also had a question. Where could he change paper money for real money, gold?

"Where'd you get paper money?" asked Remo.

"It's mine," said Chiun.

"Where? You picked it up in that poolroom in East St. Louis, didn't you?"

"It belongs to me," said Chiun.

"You played pool for it, didn't you? Didn't you? You gambled."

"I did not gamble. I educated."

"I remember this big harangue you gave me once. The wasting of my talents on games. How when you put your skills to something frivolous, you lose your skills. I mean, you made it sound like I was betraying Sinanju itself. You even told me about your teacher and the balls that could go in all directions. I remember that. I was never to use my skills in gambling."

"There is nothing worse," said Chiun solemnly, "than a talky white man." And he would say no more on the subject.

It was not hard to find Jordan. Remo told one of the girls handing out Wondergrain brochures that he was a magazine writer and he wanted to see Jordan.

Jordan came trotting, fuschia Palm Beach suit, a tie of woven mud and silver, capped teeth, and plastic black hair, wondering in basso profundo how best he could be of service. Remo wanted an interview.

"Mr. Fielding, the great agricultural genius of our times, is busy now but you can see him after *NBC News* tonight. As of today, you will be speaking to a world figure. That's the whole world."

"The round one?" said Chiun, folding his long hands before himself.

"I want to talk to you, not Mr. Fielding," said Remo.

"Anything to be of help. Mr. Fielding will be ready at 8:30 tonight after his worldwide exposure on NBC. I must run now."

But Jordan did not run far. In fact, he did not run at all. Something was holding the padded shoulder of his fuschia jacket.

"Oh, me. You want to interview me. Fine," said Jordan.

A loudspeaker crackled with a Western voice explaining the limitations of available land as Remo went with Jordan into the smaller of two tents, used as a press shed. Chiun stayed to hear the lecture because, as he explained, he was an expert on starving peoples. Just fifteen hundred years ago . . . .

Two reporters hung, passed out drunk, over a small couch near the press bar. The bartender washed glasses. Remo refused an offered drink and sat down with Jordan across from a typewriter.

"Ask away. I'm at your disposal," said Jordan.

"You most certainly are, Giordano," said Remo. "Why did you have those commodities men killed?"

"I beg your pardon," said Jordan, his black eyes blinking under indoor fluorescent.

"Why did you have Willoughby killed?"

"Willoughby who?" said Jordan evenly.

Remo pressured a knee cap.

"Eeeeow," Jordan wheezed.

The reporters woke up and seeing it was just a simple assault went back to sleep. The bartender, a giant of a man with shoulders like doorways, leaped over the bar with a thick three-foot wooden stick. With a massive swing from his heels he brought the club down on Mr. Jordan's assailant. There was a resounding crack. The crack was the stick; the head was still untouched. The bartender brought a fist smashing toward the assailant's face. The fist felt like it was deflected by a small gust of air and then there was a very funny sting under the bartender's nose and he felt very much like going to sleep. He did, underneath a desk.

"You didn't answer me," said Remo.

"Right," said Jordan. "Answer you. Answer you. Willoughby. I seem to remember the man. Commodities man. Willoughby."

"Why did you have him killed?"

"Is he dead?" said Jordan, massaging his knee.

"Very," said Remo.

"The good die young," said Jordan.

Remo put a thumb on Jordan's throat. It brought the truth out of the man. Gagging, but the truth. Willoughby was killed because he was threatening the greatest agricultural advance in the history of mankind. In the history of mankind.

"What other history is there?" asked Remo.

Willoughby had evidence that the grain market was artificially depressed. Willoughby did not know why but he suspected something big. It was hard to breathe. Would the stranger release his throat grip?

"Whew," said Jordan getting all the oxygen he needed. "Thank you," he said and straightened his tie and brushed flat his fuschia suit. "Vito, Al," he yelled. "Will you come here a minute?" And to Remo he confided they could help explain some things. Willoughby wasn't the only one, nor were there just commodities brokers. There were some construction men too. And oh, yes, said Jordan when two large men in silk suits with heavy bulges at the shoulders entered, there would soon be a reporter who couldn't keep his hands to himself.

Hearing "hands to himself" one of the reporters in a boozy slumber said, "I'm sorry, Mabel. You've got to realize I respect you as a person."

"Vito, Al. Kill this sonuvabitch," said Jordan.

"Right here, Mr. Jordan?" said Al, drawing a large square .45 with pearl insets on the handle.

"Yes."

"In front of the reporters?"

"They've passed out," said Jordan.

"You said it, boss," said Vito. "Maybe we should use a silencer?"

"Good idea," said Jordan, hobbling to his men. "I have important things to do. Don't worry about police. It's self-defense. Defend yourselves."

Remo idly listened to this, drumming on a typewriter roll with his fingertips, legs crossed, leaning back in a chair. When Al aimed the bolstered barrel of a small automatic at him, Remo centered his weight and just in case Chiun might be looking into the press tent, he kept his left wrist very straight behind the typewriter carriage. He had one worry. The chair. But as his spine pressed down suddenly into the chair, it held. That was good. And his left hand was perfectly straight from palm to forearm.

Al was squeezing the trigger when he saw and felt simultaneously the silenced automatic come back into his chest along with something else. It was heavy. He felt himself jammed into a desk. A Royal Standard was in his chest along with, he guessed, the automatic. At least that was where his arm ended and the last time he had seen the gun a fraction of a second before. The return arm of the carriage was jammed into his right ear. The black roller was into where his nose bone had been. He found breathing impossible, largely because his right lung was flat. Which was all right too because the heart didn't need oxygen anymore since his left aorta supplied only a space bar and the right ventricle ended at "D," "F," and "G."

"Keep down the frigging noise, will you?" said one of the reporters. "I'm trying to work." The reporter rolled over on a desk, fluffing a raincoat for a softer rest for his head.

"Jeez," said Vito.

He said it again. "Oh, Jeez," and without silencer he squeezed the trigger of his .45 and kept on squeezing. Unfortunately his target had moved. So had the .45. It was in his mouth and before everything went black forever, which was very quickly, he was amazed at how little it hurt. Sort of one loud sting in the back of his head.

Jordan watched the back of Vito's head splatter against the new fuchsia suit and onto the imported tie with the silver and mud weave.

"We should talk," said Jordan. "Let us reason together."

"Am I correct in assuming you had those commodities people killed because they knew about efforts to depress the market in wheat, winter wheat to be exact?"

"Correct. Absolutely. Totally correct. Totally."

"And that was so that people would invest in this new Wondergrain, because of the larger need now?"

"Make people more responsive. Correct. Totally correct. Greater need. Greater buying. It's going to be a boon to mankind. A boon. A helpful boon. Totally a boon. I can cut you in. You'll be rich beyond your wildest dreams."

"And Fielding?"

"He's an idiot," said Jordan. "We can control the whole thing. That dummy wanted to give away the profits. Name the grain after his dingy butler. It was I who saw the whole thing as Wondergrain, the miracle answer to today's food problems. I took over the packaging and marketing. I control the shares. We can be rich. Rich. Rich." Jordan screamed the "rich."

Most men scream when their spinal column snaps into their navel.

If Remo had thought only about what Jordan was saying and let his body flow the stroke, there would would have been no problem. If he had thought about just the stroke, there would have been no problem. But thinking about both, Remo noticed something wrong. Not that the final effect was different. Jordan lay on the press tent floor, ears at heel like a folded card.

It was the performance that was wrong, the angle of penetration that lacked the perfect perpendicular to his upper arm, which now felt a small meaningless twinge. The difference between Sinanju and other methods, other methods of anything for that matter, was that the form must be precisely correct, no matter what the result.

As Chiun had said: "When the results are different, it is too late." So Remo did the stroke twice more around an imaginary Jordan, the flat hand tip coming back towards itself in the snap that became perpendicular on final impact. It was right. Good.

"Disgrace," came the squeaky Oriental voice from the flap of the tent. "Now you learn to do it right. Now you bother to learn correctness. You have shamed me." It was Chiun.

"In front of whom? Who the hell else would know?" said Remo.

"Imperfection is its own disgrace," said Chiun. And then in Korean bewailing the years of pearls cast before ungrateful pale pieces of pig's ear and how not even the Master of Sinanju could transform mud into diamonds.

"No," said Chiun to someone behind him. "Do not come in. You should not look upon shame."

A telephone rang behind Remo. A reporter stirred, woke up, and answered it groggily.

"Yeah. Right. It's me. I'm right on top of everything. Yeah. They planted the grain this morning under sparkling hot skies, the new Wondergrain that can save the world from starvation, according to James O. Fielding, 42, of Denver. Yeah. Let the lead stand. Nothing happening. I'll stay right on it. Right. Harvest will be in four weeks . . . the Wondergrain. It's rough out here in the Mojave. Let me tell you. Change that lead to 'planted the grain in the dry unyielding sand of the Mojave Desert.' Etcetera. Etcetera. Right." The reporter hung up and crawled over his raincoat to the bar, where he poured a full glass of Hennessey cognac, drank two gulps, and went slowly to the floor head first so that he was sleeping upside down.

"It is CIA plot," came a woman's voice behind Chiun.

She was beautiful standing there in the desert sunlight, rich black hair flowing to her shoulders, full womanly breasts and a face of jeweled perfection, eyes dark like an unlit universe, and skin smooth with youth. She also had a mouth. Loud.

"Is CIA plot. I know. CIA plot. CIA ruining goodwill of American peoples, attempting to destroy the revolution. Hello, my name is Maria Gonzales. Long live the revolution."

"Who is this?" Remo asked Chiun.

"A brave young girl helping revolution against white imperialist oppressors," said Chiun sweetly.

"You tell her who you work for?"

"He is a revolutionary. All third-world peoples are revolutionary," said Maria.

"Could you put aside that revolutionary jazz while you're with me?" said Remo.

"As a matter of fact, yes. I am a farmer first. I talk revolution like you talk apple pie. If you are a friend of this sweet old gentleman, I'm really glad to meet you." She extended a hand. Remo took it. The palm was soft and warm. She smiled. Remo smiled. Chiun slapped the hands apart. Such touching was improper in public.

"I'm an agricultural representative of the democratic government of Free Cuba. I think you people really have something good here," said Maria. She smiled. Remo smiled back. Chiun got between them.

Fielding was pressing the final soybean into the crusty dry soil when Remo got to the inner edge of the crowd. The field itself was on top of a small hill. While the planting area was no more than twenty yards square, it sat inside an open area four times that size, surrounded by high, barbed-wire-crowned hurricane fencing. The field had a strange smell to Remo, a slight odor that was more a memory than a sense.

"Tomorrow," Fielding was saying, "I will plant a similar crop in Bangor, Maine, and the next day in the Sierras, and the following day, the final planting in Ohio. You are welcome to attend those also."

After he covered the last seed with his foot, he straightened up and rubbed his back. "Now, the sun filter," said Fielding and the workmen covered the plot with an opaque plastic tarpaulin, shaped like a tent.

"What you have just seen," said Fielding, catching his breath, "is the most significant advance in agriculture since the plow. I will tell you this. It is chemical. It eliminates the need for expensive land preparation, it expands the parameters of temperature and water needs which has kept tillable land at only a small percentage of the earth's surface. It requires no fertilizer or pesticides. It will grow in thirty days and I hope you will all be back here that day to witness this revolution. Gentlemen, you are seeing an end to world hunger."

There was a scattering of applause from foreign newsmen, some mumbling about whether this would be ten or fifteen seconds on national television, and then from the press shed came a shriek.

"Dead men. There are dead men all over the place. A massacre."

"Wow," said a reporter near Remo and Maria. "A real story now. I'm always lucky. Send me to a nothing story and I always luck out."

Like seepage from a ruptured water tank, the mob flowed toward the press shed trailing television cables. A turbaned man, with a nameplate that said "Agriculture India" tugged at Remo's arm.

"Kind sir, does this mean I do not collect my money for attending?"

"I dunno," said Remo. "I don't work here."

"I took a trip for nothing, then. For nothing. Promised two thousand dollars and will receive nothing. Western lies and hypocrisy," he said in his Indian singsong, the language of a people Chiun had once said had only two consistent traits: hypocrisy and starvation.

Sweat beaded on the patrician face of James Orayo Fielding as he watched the press disappear from the Mojave compound, heading for the twin tents outside the perimeter fence. Suddenly, it appeared as if his entire life descended on him with fatigue and he reached out for a steady arm. He grabbed for support a thin young man with high cheekbones and thick wrists. It was Remo.

"Your friends are gone," said Remo.

"The news mentality," said Maria. "In Cuba we do not allow journalists to cater to such morbid curiosity."

"Sure," said Remo. "That's because murder is an everyday thing."

"You're being unfair," said Maria.

"It is hard to make an American fair," said Chiun. "It is a thing I have been trying to teach him, lo these many years."

"Korean fairness, Little Father?" said Remo, laughing.

Chiun did not think that was funny, nor did Maria. Fielding steadied himself. Weakly he took a pill from his shirt pocket and swallowed it dry.

Remo's eyes signaled ever so briefly for Chiun to get Maria out of hearing range. Chiun suddenly noticed a vision of hibiscus, lo, across the desert, like rising zephyrs above the Katmandu Gardens. Had Maria ever seen the Katmandu gardens when the sun was mellow and the river cool like a gentle breath of a friendly north wind? In an instant, Chiun had her walking out into the desert aimlessly.

"You have very unnice friends," said Remo to Fielding.

"What do you mean?"

"Your friends kill people."

"Those deaths in the shed that everyone's yelling about?"

"Others," said Remo. "Commodities men. Construction men."

"What?" said Fielding. He was feeling weak, he said.

"Feel stronger or you'll go the way of your soybean.

76

Planted." But Fielding collapsed and Remo could tell it was not an act.

Remo carried Fielding to a small shack built inside the fenced compound for security guards and there, Fielding recovered and told Remo how he had discovered a grain process that could end starvation, could literally end hunger and want. All his troubles had started when he discovered this. Yes, he knew about the commodities men. He knew about the depressed grain market.

"I told them, I told Jordan, we didn't need that sort of help. The Oliver method, as I called it—now it's Wondergrain—it didn't need artificial help. It would replace other grains naturally because it's better. But they wouldn't listen to me. I don't even own the company anymore. I'll show you the papers. Greed has ruined us. Millions will starve because of greed. I'm going to have to go to court, won't I?"

"I guess," said Remo.

"All I need is four months. Then I'm willing to go to jail for life or whatever. Just four months and I can make the most significant contribution to mankind, ever."

"Four months?" asked Remo.

"But that won't do any good," said Fielding.

"Why not?"

"Because people have been trying to stop me since I started. Did I say four months? Well, really I don't need that. Just a month. Just thirty days until the miracle grain comes up. Then the whole world will plant it. They will throw out their old crops and put in the new feed for mankind. I know it."

"I'm not in the food business," said Remo. But what the man said haunted him and he sneaked some seeds from the briefcase of James Orayo Fielding and told him he might be able to help.

"How?" asked Fielding.

"We'll see," said Remo who that afternoon checked out two things. One, according to a botanist, was that the seeds were real. The second, according to a city clerk in the Denver municipal building, Feldman, O'Connor and Jordan now owned the controlling shares of the corporation which had rights to Wondergrain, as of a date three months and sixteen days in the future.

As Remo explained to Chiun that night:

"Little Father, I have a chance to do something really good for the world. This man is honest."

"For one to do what he knows, is good," said Chiun. "That is all the good any man can do. All else is ignorance."

"No," said Remo. "I can save the world."

And to this the Master of Sinanju shook his head sadly.

"In our records, my son, we know that those who would make heaven tomorrow make hell today. All the robbers who ever stole and all the conquerers who ever conquered and all the petty evil men who preyed on the helpless have not, in their counted history, caused as much massive grief as one man who attempts to save mankind and gets others to follow him."

"But I don't need others," said Remo.

"So much the worse," said the Master of Sinanju.

CHAPTER SIX

Johnny "Deuce" Deussio saw it on television while waiting for the Johnny Carson show. It was the late-night action news. Johnny Deuce always watched it between his feet. Beth Marie did her nails. She had so many curlers and pins and rods in her starkly blonde hair that Johnny Deuce long ago stopped making advances to her. It was too much like loving an erector set with cream.

Beth Marie did not complain. She thought it was nice, in fact, and that Johnny was becoming more gentlemanly. The bed came around their feet in a circle. To his left was the light panel indicating the electronic security systems were working. It also had an open phone to his cousin, Sally. Because of the dream that night, he now had a small-caliber pistol tucked near the control panel.

Beth Marie lathered cream on her face to his right. He fingered the panel a lot while watching late night action news, starring Gil Braddigan, anchorman. Unlike many other newsmen of St. Louis, Braddigan did not require little gifts to do favors. He didn't know enough to be bought off. Beth Marie thought Braddigan was sexy. Johnny Deuce did not tell her that Braddigan was a flaming fag. You didn't use that kind of language to your wife in bed.

"I think he's sexy," said Beth Marie, as Braddigan rode the television into their bedroom with manicured face, hair, smile, and voice. Johnny Deuce fingered the rising edge of the plastic call buttons on the panel. He hoped Johnny Carson wouldn't unload another rerun or have that squeaky-voiced writer as moderator. Johnny Deuce did not like to fall asleep without the sounds of friendly voices.

"Terrible," said Beth Marie.

"Huh?" said Johnny Deuce.

"Three men were mauled to death in some vegetable laboratory. Out in the desert."

"Too bad," said Deussio. He was thinking about business. His secretary had nice legs. She had nice breasts and a nice duff. She had a sweet face. She wanted Deussio to get a divorce. Even though she worked in only the legitimate fronts of Deussio enterprises, she knew too much already. She had threatened that either she got Deussio in marriage or she would leave. This was not a major business decision. It was a simple one. If she left, her next residence would be the bottom of the Missouri with concrete panty hose over that lovely duff. Such was life. Deussio was startled to feel Beth Marie touch him. In bed no less.

"They found one guy in this press room with a typewriter mashed into his chest," she said.

"Awful," said Deussio. Willie "Pans" Panzini was another matter. He was spending too much money on

80

what Deussio was paying him. This meant that Willie Pans was either stealing from Deussio, which was bad and could be corrected by a firm lecture or some moderate grief, or he was collecting money on his own from other sources, which would be nonnegotiably terminal. Sally would have to find out which. Perhaps stick a blowtorch in Willie Pans's face. Blowtorches brought the truth out of people.

"Another man had his back broken. A whole piece of his spine went right through his stomach. That's what the coroner out there said," Beth Marie said.

"Awful," said Deussio.

"I think we knew him. We knew the man. We saw him last year when we went to the coast. That lovely public relations person."

"What?" said Deussio sitting up in bed.

"All those killings. Your friend James Jordan was killed today at some vegetable experiment."

"Wondergrain?"

"That's right."

"Jeeez," said Deussio, grabbing Beth Marie's shoulders and demanding she repeat everything Gil Braddigan had said about the desert killings. This was much like getting a stock market report told to a social worker and filtered through a retard. All he got was intimations of something horrible happening to their friend Jordan whose wife had set such a nice spread in their Carmel home. As Deussio listened and questioned he began to wonder.

"Thanks," he said, leaving the bed and ringing for Sally.

"John," said Beth Marie.

"What?"

"You want to?"

"Want to what?"

"You know what," said Beth Marie. "That."

"That's some way for a wife of eighteen years to talk," said Deussio and met Sally running up the hallway with a drawn snub-nosed .38.

He slapped Sally in the face.

"Dummy," said Johnny Deuce.

"What I do? What I do?"

And for that Johnny Deuce hit harder. The smack echoed down the hallway.

"Will you shut up out there, I'm trying to watch TV," came Beth Marie's voice.

"Why didn't you tell me about Giordano, out-on-the-coast Giordano?"

"What Giordano?"

"Giordano who was killed today. Dreaming, huh? I was dreaming that last time, huh? Dreaming. Those guys was frigging crushed to death."

"I didn't hear nothing."

"Don't we get word no more? What is this? I could be killed in my sleep. Dreaming, huh? I ain't sleeping in this house. We're going to the mattresses," said Deussio, meaning his crime family was preparing for war.

"Against who?" said Sally.

"Against what, you mean," said Johnny Deuce. "Against what."

"Yeah. What?"

"We don't know what, dummy," said Johnny Deuce and he slapped Sally hard in the face and when Beth Marie complained again about the noise in the hall, he told her to go finger herself. Sally did not protest the slapping assaults against his pride. The closer one got to John Deussio, the less one became affronted by his famous temper and the more one appreciated an artist.

Deussio had raised the level of mob war in the midwest to exquisite craftsmanship. Neat surgical strikes that took out precise portions of organizations and left profits undisturbed.

A group of bookmakers on Front Street in Marietta, Ohio, who thought profits did not have to be shared totally with St. Louis connections, learned one night the folly of independence. Each one found himself in a warehouse, tied but not gagged. In this way, he was able to hear the shock sounds of friends he knew. In the center of the warehouse was a man stripped nude. When a spotlight flashed on his face, they saw it had been the man who had promised them protection from St. Louis for a far smaller cut than they had been paying St. Louis. The man was swinging from a rope. The searchlight lowered and they saw a reddish wet cavity where his stomach had been. They heard their own groans and sobs and then the lights went off and they were all in darkness.

One by one, each felt a cold edge of a knife press against his solar plexus, felt his shirt buttons be unbuttoned, and waited. And nothing happened. They were escorted out of the warehouses, untied, and taken, shaking, to a hotel suite where food was laid out in abundance. No one was hungry. A fat man with stains on his shirt and great difficulty in speaking English introducted himself as Guglielmo Balunta; he worked for people in St. Louis who provided these gentlemen services and he wished, what was the word for it, to toast their health and prosperity. Excuse his poor English.

He was worried, he said, because animals were about. They did awful things. They were not businessmen like him and his guests. All they knew was kill.

Cut stomachs and things. This did not help business, did it? Everyone in the room assured Balunta it sure as hell didn't. No.

But Balunta had a problem. If he couldn't return to St. Louis and assure his people that they would get their cut, they would not listen to him. These animals always have their ears for violence. He needed to bring something home, he said, some pledge of good faith, that business would continue as usual. Maybe a little better than usual.

Men who just minutes before could not control bowel or bladder assured their host he spoke very good English even if all the words were not in English. The increased cut, well, yes, it seemed reasonable. Fear made many previously unacceptable things reasonable.

The success of this was only a small part of Johnny Deuce's genius. For not only had he arranged it that not one bookmaker was hurt and thus no profits were lost for the day but he saw great possibilities and he shared his reasoning with Guglielmo Balunta. They spoke in a Sicilian dialect, although Johnny's was not good, having only learned it from his parents.

There were times, said Johnny Deuce, that offered incredible opportunities, just because no one else had thought of them. Balunta waved his hands, indicating he did not understand. Johnny, driving their car back to St. Louis—he had asked to take Balunta alone personally—had difficulty talking with both hands on the wheel, but he continued.

Balunta was in for a very nice cut of the increase from the gambling in Marietta. Not much. But enough of a *causa bono* for contentment.

Balunta assured Johnny Deuce that he too would be rewarded for his brilliant work. Johnny Deuce said this was not the point. Who was the one man in the organization most trusted now by the top man in St. Louis? It was Balunta, of course. He had just done a good job.

But some day, Johnny reasoned, Balunta would be offended by what was given him. Some day he would be cut out of something that belonged to him. Some day he would have grievance against his boss.

Balunta said this would never happen. He was close with the don. And he held up two stubby fingers. Especially now that he had brought this small southern Ohio town into line so neatly. Especially now.

"No," said Johnny Deuce. "I am young and you are old but I know as surely as the sun rises that disagreements occur in business." And he named incidents and he named names and even pointed out that Balunta had gotten his own position because his predecessor had had to be eliminated.

This was true, admitted Balunta. And it was here that Deussio's strategic brilliance began to show. When you have this disagreement or trouble, or even when they are on the horizon, how hard will it be to get to the top people? And when he said "get to" he took one hand off the wheel and pointed it as if it were a gun.

Very hard, agreed Balunta. He conceded that they might even get to him first. In fact, probably. Which was what kept most people in line.

"Now tell me," said Deussio, "what does the horizon look like now. You said it yourself. Clear."

"You're the guy coming home with the bacon," he said, lapsing into English. "You're the guy who's due a bigger cut. You're the fucking hero."

"So what you saying, Johnny Deuce?" asked Balunta.

"We hit the top now."

"Mi Dio," said Balunta. "This is a big thing. Too big."

"It's either you hit them now while you got the advantage or they get you when they have it. I admit, it's a hard choice. But you do the hard thing today when it's easy or you take the hard thing in the face tomorrow. When it's tough. Frigging tough. You know I'm right."

Balunta was quiet as the car went through the countryside. And Johnny Deuce further showed his genius, a genius that would give most of the midwest mob quiet for more than a decade.

He began by telling Balunta he knew what Balunta was thinking. If this young man is willing to have me go against my boss now, wouldn't he, at the moment of success, do the same thing to me?

Balunta said he was thinking no such thing.

"But I would be foolish," continued Johnny Deuce. "If I go against you, then my number two would see this and go against me. Now if I do not go against you, my number two will worry what you will do if he succeeds with me. I am the only one who can stop what I have started and I have a vested interest in doing so. You are going to give me a very big piece of the action from the outset. A very big piece. Together we have no worries. We will work things out for both our safeties."

But everyone, Balunta pointed out, wants it all.

"Everyone who doesn't know that all of it is a one-way ticket to the marble orchard," said Johnny Deuce. "You'll see. It'll work if we share. If we share, we're strong."

"Mi Dio," said Balunta and Deussio knew that this was a "yes." For ten days, bodies turned up downstream in the Missouri, shotguns bloomed from the front win-

dows of cars, brains were blown into dinner *linguine*. Deussio struck so fast and so quickly it was only when the St. Louis wars, as they were later called, were over that those who mattered knew where the killing had come from. And by that time, it was Don Guglielmo Balunta.

Johnny Deuce's talents and his proven loyalty created a new order from St. Louis to Omaha. Such was Don Guglielmo's trust in his young genius that when others would come to him with stories of the crazy things that Johnny Deuce did, Don Guglielmo would say:

"My Johnny does crazy things today that come out smart tomorrow." When he hired the electronics experts, people hinted he was crazy. When he hired the funny Orientals, people whispered he was crazy. When he hired computer programmers, people said he was crazy. And each time, Don Guglielmo Balunta would answer that his Johnny would be proven smart tomorrow. Even when the word got around about his strange dream and how he had young athletes try to climb up to an impossible-to-reach window in his home, even then Don Guglielmo told everyone his Johnny would be proven smart tomorrow.

But when Johnny started ordering everyone to go to the mattresses when there was no enemy in sight, Don Guglielmo was instantly worried. He did not even have to send for Johnny Deuce. Johnny came himself, with no bodyguard and a very fat briefcase.

Johnny was paunchier now than in those early years when first the two had assumed control. His hair surrendered to shiny scalp along a thinning line of resistance. His face had lost the hard lines to a smothering layer of flesh but the dark eyes still shone with sharp fury.

87

Don Guglielmo, in a ruby smoking jacket, lounged on the edge of a plush green couch set on what appeared to be acres of marble flooring. Johnny Deuce sat on the edge of his chair, his feet planted forward, his knees together, refusing a glass of strega, a piece of fruit, talk of weather and family. He told his don he was worried.

Over the years Don Guglielmo would listen very carefully but this time his hands raised and he said he would hear none of it.

"This time," said Balunta, "you listen to me. I am more worried than you. You listen. I talk. You go to the Miami Beach. You get the sun. You get the rest. You get yourself a girl with those nice titties that go up. You have wine. You eat the good food. You get sun. Then we talk."

"*Patron,* we face the most deadly enemy. Deadliest ever."

"Where?" said Balunta, his hands rising to the heavens. "Show me this enemy. Where is he?"

"He is on the horizon. I've done a lot of thinking. There's something going on in this country that eventually means the end of us all. All of us. The organization. Everything. Not just here but all over. It's not just that bad night I had. That was just the tip of an iceberg that's going to destroy us all."

Don Guglilmo leaped from the sofa and grabbed Johnny Deuce's head in his hands. Palms to ears, he raised Deussio's head so their eyes must meet.

"You get the rest. You get the rest now. No more talk. You listen to your don. You get the rest. No more talk. After you rest, we talk. Okay? Okay?"

"As you say," said Johnny Deuce.

"Atsa good. I worry for you," said Balunta.

And Johnny Deuce told his don he could use a drink but not the bought stuff. Good red wine made especially for the don. And wine was brought in in a large green gallon jug and placed on the slate-gray table top. Deussio placed a hand over his glass and did not raise it.

"You won't take the drink with your don?"

Johnny Deuce removed his hand from the cut crystal glass.

"The worries are in your head. You think your don would poison his right arm?" said Balunta. "Would I poison my heart? My brains? You are the legs of my throne. Never. Never." And to show his good faith, Balunta took the glass sitting before his Johnny and drank it all. Then he threw the glass toward the wall but it fell short, cracking on the marble floor.

"I knew you wouldn't poison me, Don Guglielmo," said Deussio.

"Then why you no drink the wine with your don?"

Guglielmo Balunta wanted to express himself with his hands. Wanted to throw them out wide to express his confusion. But they did not move very well. They felt icy and they stung gently as if immersed in fresh Vichy water. He felt giddy and light. When he stepped back to the couch the legs did not step with him. So he went back anyway and almost reached the couch. The fall seemed far away, not hurting as a collapse on marble usually did but rather a gentle laying down so that he was looking up at his beautiful ceiling. His Johnny was saying something. He kept talking about inevitabilities and rolled from his briefcase that funny long paper with the holes in it. Guglielmo Balunta did not care. He thought of a very white little rock he once had near

Messina where he was born. He had thrown it down into the narrow straits that separated Sicily from Italy and told his friends: "I will live until the sea gives up that rock." He thought about his youth and then saw a vision of the straits of Messina. Something white was coming up through the waves. A speck. No. His rock.

Johnny Deuce did not know for sure if Don Guglielmo could hear him. Sally and the other men were already coming through the outside gate of the Balunta estate. Balunta's household men would be sent to a small regime in Detroit. They would not fight if the don were dead because there was no one left to fight for. However, if Johnny were alone and standing over the corpse, they might take out their rage of their own failure on him. So it would be quick. And in case his don could still hear him, he wanted him to know why he had to kill him.

"This sheet is the figuring of several years. Things are happening in this country that have no reason to happen. I saw it several years ago when Scubisci had his troubles in the east. We called this 'no reason' the X-factor. And we said this "no reason" is a reason. So all of a sudden a tight city becomes untight and politicians and police are going to jail all of a sudden with prosecutors having evidence they shouldn't have. Judges we've owned for years suddenly terrorized by some other force. That force is the X-factor, and if you look at it, you'll realize we're through. In ten or fifteen years, we're not going to be able to do business."

Sally was past the front doors with his own men and their weapons came out. There was murmuring in the hallway outside the vast marble-flooring living room and Johnny Deuce called everyone inside.

"Heart attack," he said, keeping the computer print-outs concealed against his side, even though he knew the bodyguards would no more understand them than Balunta did.

"Yeah. Heart attack," said one of the house body-guards and Johnny Deuce nodded for Sally to take them out of the room. On the way out, one of the guards whispered to Sally: "What is he, talking to a stiff?" And Sally cuffed him in the back of the head and the body-guard understood that.

Deussio continued in the empty room. He told his dead don that the X-factor was a force that was making government work, not for those who tried to buy it but for those who voted for it. And this X-factor was grow-ing stronger. Therefore every day an attack was de-layed, the chances of overcoming X-factor grew smaller. By the time someone with Balunta's mentality had been ready to move, it would be too late.

The enforcer unit of this X-factor had brushed through St. Louis a few days before, just an edge of the iceberg. It was after something else at the time.

"We have one small advantage and I'm going to use it," said Deussio. "The X-factor does not know we un-derstand it. See here. Look."

And he unfolded the long computer printout listing probabilities. Even if Don Guglielmo had been breath-ing, he would have understood it no better. Which was why he had to die. The strategist, John Vincent Deus-sio, knew he had to move now, even if others didn't. Which made him what he was. Which made him very dangerous. Unlike the others, he knew he was in a war for survival. So he felt very free to kill anyone who would not aid the cause.

He drank the unpoisoned wine Balunta had poured for himself, the wine into which Johnny had not dropped the poison pellet, and sat back on the sofa to prepare his attack.

CHAPTER SEVEN

The first Remo saw the rough sketch of himself was at the Ohio demonstration. The surrounding fields were green with corn and Fielding had explained that he also had to show the process worked in good, moderate-climate soil as well as bad. The field was raised on a little hill surrounded by a chain-link fence.

Maria Gonzales, carrying a Russian passport because her country did not have relations with the United States, spoke with a French agronomist who noted his country had large farming sections with climate and soil like Ohio.

Chiun engaged several cameramen from television networks, asking why there was so much violence and filth in daytime dramas nowadays. Obviously one had replied with a sharp answer because Remo saw ambulance attendants lifting the portable TV camera from a man's shoulder and placing him on a stretcher.

Newsmen worked in shirt sleeves. The Miami County Sheriff's office wore open-necked short-sleeved shirts and carried heavy sidearms, the sheriff having vowed that there would be no Mojave-type incident here in Piqua, Ohio.

"We're not like those people out there," said the sheriff.

"Out where?" asked a reporter.

"Out anywhere," said the sheriff. Sweat ran down his face like glycerin beads over packaged lard. Remo scanned the crowd looking for any possible attack on Fielding. He caught Maria's eye. She smiled. He smiled back. Chiun walked between them.

A soft breeze caught the corn in a neighboring field and made the lazy summer day smell like life itself. Remo caught an exchange of glances between a man in a Palm Beach hat and another in a gray light summer suit. They were across the field from each other. And both looked at a paunchy man with large shoulders who glanced at something in his hands, then looked at Remo. When Remo looked back, the man tucked the object into his trousers pocket and became very interested in what was happening in the field. The three men had the field triangulated. Remo sidled to the paunchy man in the white suit.

"Hi," said Remo. "I'm a pickpocket."

The man stared straight ahead.

"I said hello," said Remo. The man's alligator shoes pressed into the newly turned Ohio soil under the weight of 280 pounds of muscles and flesh and a two-day growth. He had a face that had been banged here and there by fist and club and a whitish lumpy line which was the completed healing process of a long-ago blade. He was slightly taller than Remo and had shoulders and wide fists that had obviously done some banging themselves. His body oozed the odor of yesterday's scotch and today's sirloin.

"I said hello," said Remo again.

"Uh, hello," said the man.

"I'm a pickpocket," Remo repeated. The man's hairy heavy hand moved down to his right trouser pocket.

"Thank you for showing me which pocket I should pick," said Remo.

"What?" said the man and Remo cut two fingers down between fatty palm and hefty hip, making a neat tearing slice down the right side of the man's trousers.

"What?" grunted the man who suddenly felt his undershorts under his right palm. He grabbed for the skinny guy but when his huge hands closed on the shoulders, the shoulders were not there and the skinny guy kept on walking and looking through the trouser pocket as if strolling through a garden reading a book.

"Hey, you. Gimme back my pocket," said the man. "That's my pocket." He swung at the back of the head but the skinny guy's head was just not there. It didn't jerk or duck, it was just not there as the swing went through where it was. The two other men in the triangle moved toward the commotion. The Miami County sheriff's office moved toward the commotion.

"Anything wrong?" said the sheriff, surrounded by deputies with their hands on their sidearms.

"No," said the big man with the tear in his trouser. "Nothing wrong. Nothing." He said this by instinct. He could not remember ever telling a policeman the truth.

"Anything wrong?" the sheriff asked Remo.

"No," said Remo, examining the pocket he had picked.

"All right, then," said the sheriff. "Break it up." Seeing that all his deputies were clustered around him, he yelled for them to get back to their positions. There wasn't, he said, going to be another Mojave Desert incident in this county.

Remo threw away car keys and some bills from the pocket. He held onto a small square paper that looked printed. It was a sketch of two men, the stiff expressionless lines of what might have been a police composite. An old Oriental with wispy hair and a younger Caucasian with sharp features and high cheekbones. The Caucasion had hair similar to Remo's. The Oriental's eyes were deeper than Chiun's and then Remo realized it was a composite sketch of himself and Chiun. The deeper eyes told him and told him who had stood over the artist telling him 'yes' and 'no' as eyes and mouths appeared on paper. All eyes looked deeper when there was direct above light, as over a pool table in a pool hall.

Pete's Pool Parlour in East St. Louis. The Caucasian's eyes weren't so deep set because Remo had not stood at the table. He waved to Chiun.

Chiun came in behind the two other men of the triangle.

"Look," said Remo, showing the card to Chiun. "Now I know you won that money playing pool. You were at the pool table. Look at the eyes."

The man in the Palm Beach hat whispered something about having somebody. The big man trotted to a white Eldorado at the edge of the crowd.

"The shading of the eyes. Yes, I see," said Chiun. "The light from above."

"Right," said Remo.

The big man without the trouser pocket eased the Eldorado over the soft ground to Chiun and Remo. He threw open the driver's door, disclosing a shotgun in his lap. The door hid the gun from the sheriff's men. It pointed at Remo and Chiun.

"That could not be me," said Chiun. "It is a very close likeness of you considering it was obviously painted from memory. It lacks the character I put into your face. The other person is a stranger to me."

"Looks just like the gook," said the man in the Palm Beach hat, coming up behind them. "We got 'em. You two, get in that car and move quietly."

"This could not be my face," said Chiun. "This is the face of an old man. It could not be me. It lacks warmth and joy and beauty. It lacks the grace of character. It lacks the countenance of majesty. This is just the face of an old man." He looked up to the man in the Palm Beach hat. "However, if you could give me a large size of the white man, I would like to have it framed."

"Sure, old man," said the man in the Palm Beach hat. "How big? Eight by ten?"

"No. Not that big. My picture of Rad Rex is an eight-by-ten. Something smaller. To stand near my picture of Rad Rex, but slightly behind it. Do you know that Rad Rex, the famous television actor, called me gracious and humble?"

His face sparkled with pride.

"All right," said the man with a tight-lipped smile. "You got an eight-by-ten of a fag, I'll print you one of these but smaller."

"What is it, this fag?" Chiun asked Remo.

Remo sighed. "It is a boy who likes boys."

"A pervert?" asked Chiun.

"He thinks so," said Remo.

"A dirty disgusting thing?" asked Chiun.

"Depends on how you look at it."

"The way this creature—"Chiun jerked his head toward the man in the Palm Beach hat—"looks at it."

"The way he looks at it," Remo said. "Right, dirty and disgusting."

"I thought as much," said Chiun. He turned to the man in the hat who had begun to wonder why Johnny Deussio was sending all the way to Ohio to collect a couple of half-decks where there was no shortage of the mentally ill back home in St. Louis.

"You. Come here," said Chiun.

"Get in the car," said the man with the hat. Enough was enough.

"After you," said Chiun and the man with the Palm Beach hat did not notice anything and did not really feel anything and then he was being propelled over the old man's head, toward the open waiting door of the car. He slammed into its front seat. His head hit the head of the driver and his body slammed down atop the barrel of the shotgun. The driver's head snapped back and his finger jerked the trigger involuntarily. The shotgun went off with a muffled roar.

A red whoosh of flame darted out of the car. Pellets kicked up dirt around Remo and Chiun's feet.

"Hey, fella, careful," said Remo. "Somebody could get hurt." He turned around to see if anyone had paid attention to the shotgun blast. The third man was now standing behind him, a .45 in his hand.

"In the car."

"In the car?" said Remo. "Right, in the car."

The third man went over Remo's head and landed atop the other two hulks in the front seat. But Remo did not notice that because he saw two sheriff's deputies approaching him.

"Oh, oh," said Remo. "Let's get out of here. Get in the car, Chiun."

"You too?" said Chiun.

"Please, Chiun, get in the car."

"As long as you say please. Remembering that we are coequal partners."

"Right, right," said Remo.

Chiun was in the back seat of the Eldorado and Remo behind the wheel. The sheriff's deputies, he could see through the window, were closer now, starting to walk faster in the manner of police who aren't sure anything wrong has been done but by God they don't want anybody to go leaving the scene of the crime.

Remo chucked one of the groggy squirming bodies into the backseat.

"No," said Chiun firmly. "I will not have them back here."

"Why me, God?" said Remo. He shoved the remaining quarter-ton of flesh against the passenger's door, put the car in gear, and drove off. For a moment, in his rearview mirror, he could see the sheriff's men looking at him driving away, only slightly interested. Then his view was blocked as the body from the backseat was reinserted by Chiun into the front.

He drove out along a dirty road that crisscrossed through cornfields, feeling pretty good. The last Mojave demonstration by Fielding had lost much of its front-page space to the violence at the demonstration site; this time he had prevented that. It was the least one could do for a man who was going to save the world from hunger and starvation.

The man in the Palm Beach hat was the first to regain control of himself. Surprisingly, he found his gun still in his hand and he fought his way out of the mass

99

of arms and legs and pointed the automatic at Remo. "Okay, bright eyes, now pull over to the side and stop."

"Chiun," said Remo.

"No," said Chiun. "I will not soil my hands with anyone who defames the good name of Rad Rex, brilliant star of *As the Planet Revolves*."

"C'mon, Chiun, act right," Remo said.

"No."

"This isn't the one who said anything about Rad Rex," lied Remo.

"Well, you can't blame me for making such a mistake. Everybody knows all you whites look alike. But . . . ."

The man with the .45, past whom the bickering had drifted, never had an opportunity to witness its outcome. Before he could move, before he could speak again to warn this skinny punk at the wheel to pull over, there was a slight pain in his head. It never felt like more than the irritation of a mosquito's sting and he never felt anything again as Chiun's iron index finger went through his temple into his brain.

The man dropped back onto the pile of bodies.

"You lied, Remo," said Chiun. "I could tell he was the one of the evil mouth, because his head is empty."

"Never trust a white man. Particularly a coequal partner."

"Yes," said Chiun. "But as long as I am at it—" He leaned over the back of the front seat and while Remo drove, sent the other two men to join their companion, then sat back in his seat contentedly.

Remo waited until he had gotten out of sight of the demonstration area, then parked the car under a tree. He left the motor running.

"C'mon, Chiun, we'd better get back. There just

might be more back there, with Fielding as their target."

"There are no more," said Chiun.

"You can't be sure. Somehow, they made us as Fielding's bodyguards or something. Probably they think if they got rid of us, they get a clear shot at Fielding."

"There are no more," Chiun insisted. "And why would anyone attempt to harm Fielding?"

"Chiun, I don't know," said Remo. "Maybe they're trying to get the secret of Fielding's miracle grains. Steal the formulas and sell them. There are evil people in the world, you know."

"Remember you said that . . . partner," said Chiun.

CHAPTER EIGHT

The last time Johnny Deuce had looked forward with anticipation to the six o'clock news had been when the United States Senate was investigating organized crime and he'd had a chance to laugh at his old friends.

They had come on in a parade. People he had given advice to, people he had tried to straighten out, but for all the new clothes and even though they didn't carry weapons anymore and even though they had all wrapped themselves up in corporate blankets, they still had the old Mustache Pete mentality. So they wound up providing six o'clock news fodder for America while Johnny Deuce was home in his living room, trying to keep his wife's hand away from him and laughing aloud.

But this time the news was no laughing matter, not because of what was on it but because of what wasn't on it. There was a long glowing story of the Fielding demonstration in Ohio. A made-up newcaster came on in a shot taken next to the freshly planted field and talked glowingly about the great benefits to mankind from the miracle grains. He was an Ohio-based newsman and in a burst of parochial pride, he pointed out that today's planting had been a marked change from the one in the Mojave that had been sullied by still-unexplained violence.

Johnny Deuce stopped listening when the newscaster began to blather about America living up to its responsibilities to provide sustenance for the world.

He heard the weather forecast call for bad weather and then he sat in his small room thinking and it was only when the eleven o'clock news came on that he rose himself from his reverie and focused his attention again on the screen.

But there was just the same newscast. No reports of violence, no reports of Fielding's bodyguards being killed, and as he listened Johnny Deuce wasted no time coming to a truthful conclusion. The three men who had been sent to do in the hard-faced white man and the old Oriental were dead.

If they had succeeded, their work would have been on the news. That was the deductive evidence; the inductive evidence was that they had not called and Johnny Deuce had told them they had better call by seven P.M., no later, or they would have their balls filled with sand.

He let the sound of the rest of the newscast drone on as he lapsed immediately back into the rest state of the last five hours, sitting languidly while his brain whirred along, formulating his plans, setting up his attack, and this time in his mind making sure it would work.

He was satisfied and convinced and he snapped out

103

of it just long enough to catch the end of the newscast. The weatherman was on. He was a thin man with a mustache and a half-a-bag on.

The forecast was still for rain.

CHAPTER NINE

At the same time Johnny Deussio was thinking, Remo was bringing his mighty intellect to bear upon much the same problem: killing.

Who could want Fielding's formula so badly that they would try to get it by first disposing of Remo and Chiun? Since the magic Wondergrains were virtually going to be given away, who would gain by stealing their secret?

Despite the accumulated mass of scar tissue and raw knuckles that he and Chiun had been running into, Remo's instincts told him that it was not a mob venture. The mob had other things to worry about besides farming. Loan-sharking was quite profitable enough; so was prostitution, drugs, gambling, and politics, the usual kinds of crime in America.

No. Not the mob. Remo decided that some foreign power was behind the violence that seemed to dog Fielding's steps.

His first suspicion was India, but Chiun scoffed at that suggestion when Remo made it.

"India would never hire killers, even fat ones, to try to do a job. They would not want to waste a few thousand of your dollars when it could be used to help build more nuclear weapons."

"You sure?" asked Remo.

"Of course. India would try to get the formula exclusively for itself by praying for it."

Remo nodded and lay back down on the sofa in their Dayton hotel room. Who else, if not India? Who else had been at the demonstration?

Of course.

Cuba. Maria Gonzales.

"Chiun," said Remo again.

Chiun was sitting in the center of the hotel living room rug, staring at his fingertips which were steepled together.

"That is my name," he said, not taking his eyes from his fingers.

"Do you know where that Cuban woman is staying? Did she tell you?"

"I am not in the habit of finding out the hotel rooms of strange women," said Chiun.

"I don't know. You kept getting between the two of us, and I was beginning to think that maybe you were ditching Barbra Streisand for her."

"Be cautious," said Chiun, resenting any levity about the great unrequited love of his life. "Even coequal partners must speak with discretion."

"You don't know where she is?"

"She is a Cuban. If she is still in town, she will be in the cheapest hotel."

"Thank you."

106

The desk clerk downstairs told Remo that the Hotel Needham was the cheapest hotel in town. In fact, not only the cheapest but the dirtiest.

When Remo called the Hotel Needham, he found that indeed a Maria Gonzales was registered there. In fact there were three Maria Gonzaleses registered there.

"This one's kind of good-looking."

"Most of the girls registered here are kind of good-looking," said a man's oily voice over the phone. "Course it all depends on your taste. Now if you want my advice . . . ."

"No, I don't think I do. This chick would have checked in just today."

"I'm not in the habit of giving out such information," the voice said as the verbal oil congealed.

"I'm in the habit of giving out fifty-dollar bills to people who tell me what I want to know," said Remo.

"Maria Gonzales checked in today into Room 363. She's different from our other two Marias. She's a Cuban; the other two are spicks. We don't get many Cuban broads around here but I guess she hasn't had a chance to establish herself yet because there haven't been any phone calls or visits or . . . ."

"I'll be right over," said Remo. "I've got fifty for you."

"I'll wait. How will I recognize you?"

"My fly will be zipped."

The desk clerk at the Hotel Needham had looks to match his voice. He was fifty struggling to look only forty-nine; 195 dressed to look 150; short dressed to look tall, balding but coiffed to look hairy. If Brillo strands coated with spar varnish could be called hair.

"Yeah?" he said to Remo.

"I'm Pete Smith, looking for my brother John. You got a John Smith registered here?"

"Twelve of them."

"Yeah, but he'd have his wife with him," said Remo.

"All twelve," said the clerk.

"Yeah, but she's a blond in a miniskirt, good legs, big boobs, and wears too much makeup."

"Ten of them."

"She's got the clap."

"Not here," said the clerk. "This is a clean place."

"Good," said Remo. "That's really what I wanted to find out. My brother's not registered here. I just wanted to look the place over. IBM might want the grand ballroom for its next annual stockholders' meeting."

"Listen, buddy, do you want something?"

"I want to give you fifty dollars."

"I'm listening, I'm listening."

Remo peeled a fifty from a cluster of bills in his pocket and dropped it on the desk. "Maria Gonzales still in room 363?"

The clerk put the money away before answering. "Yes. Want me to announce you?"

"No, don't bother. Surprises are always such fun, aren't they?"

From inside room 363, martial music was playing. Remo knocked loudly to be heard over it.

He knocked again. The music dropped suddenly in volume. From behind the door, a voice asked: "Who is it?"

"Cuba Libre," said Remo.

The door opened cautiously, still fastened with a chain. Maria peered through the crack. Remo smiled.

"Hi. Remember me?"

"If you have come to apologize for the behavior of your countrymen, you are too late," she sputtered.

"Aaaah, what happened?" asked Remo solicitously.

She glanced downward toward Remo's groin. "At least you know how to behave yourself. You have learned manners from the grand Oriental. You may come in. But behave yourself."

"What's happened to make you mad at us?" asked Remo, stepping inside the room.

Maria was wearing the same clothes she had worn that afternoon, a khaki miniskirt and khaki blouse, both of them filled just right. She looked like a security guard at the local Playboy Club.

She turned toward Remo and put her hands on her hips in a gesture of pout. "I have been here but four hours. Already five men have been pounding on my door, demanding that I let them in. They say unspeakable things. One displayed himself."

"Exposed," corrected Remo.

"That is correct. What kind of country is this where men do that?"

"They think you're a different Maria Gonzales. A hooker."

"What is this hooker?"

"A prostitute."

"Ah, yes. The prostitutes. We had them before Fidel."

"You had sugar harvests back then too."

"Ah, but now we have the dignity."

"And the empty belly."

Maria started to answer, stopped, then nodded abruptly. "Right. And that is why I am here. And you can help me because you are a most important Yankee."

"How do you know that?"

"The Oriental. He told me, as a Third World comrade, that you were very important. You were in charge of keeping the Constitution safe. He said he was your coequal partner but no one believed he was as important as you because his skin was yellow. Are you in charge of keeping the Constitution safe?"

"Absolutely," said Remo. "I keep it in a footlocker under my bed."

"Then you must tell me how Mister Fielding does his miracle growing." Maria's face was an open appeal.

"You really want to know, don't you?"

"Yes."

"Why? Wondergrain's almost going to be given away."

"Almost is not good enough. My country is a very poor country, Remo . . . it is Remo, isn't it? Any cost is too high a cost. All our funds are committed. We owe our souls to the Russians. Can we now give our bodies to the American Yankees? That is why I was sent, to try to find out how Fielding does this thing he is going to do."

"Would you be willing to kill for it?" asked Remo.

"I would be willing to do anything for it. It is for Cuba . . . for Fidel . . . for the memory of Ché . . . for the socialist revolution."

She raised her hands and began to unbutton her khaki blouse. When it was open she pulled it back exposing her breasts. She smiled at Remo. "I would do anything for the secret. Even be your hooper."

"Hooker."

"Right. Hooker." Maria sat back onto the bed, removed her blouse, then arranged herself in a prone position as if she were setting a vase with flowers. "I

110

will be your hooker and then you will tell me your secrets. Is it a deal?"

Remo hesitated a moment. If she had killed people already to find out Fielding's secrets, why would she be trying to screw it out of Remo? On the other hand, if she had nothing to do with the killings, then Remo would be taking advantage of her by pretending to know something about the formula that he did not know.

Remo wrestled with his conscience, which maintained its unblemished scoreless record.

"You'll go to any lengths, won't you?"

"If the lengths, it is depraved, I will do it," said Maria, licking her lips as she had seen done in American films before they stopped being shown in Cuba. "I will do anything for the formula. Even go to the lengths."

Remo sighed. No wonder she and Chiun seemed to get along so well. When they chose, neither could understand English.

"All right," said Remo. "To the lengths!"

Remo figured himself a winner by at least twenty-six lengths. This was preordained by some of the first training he had received when he entered the world of CURE and Chiun.

Women, Chiun had warned Remo on that long-ago occasion, were warm-bodied animals, like cows, and as cows would give more milk if they were kept contented, women would give less aggravation if kept in the same state. However, he explained, a woman did not get contentment as a man did, through the pleasures of his intellect or his work. Women must be kept contented through heart and emotions.

"That means they're less worthy than men?" said Remo.

"That means you are stupid. No. Women are not less than men. They are different from men. In many ways, they are more than men. For instance. One can frighten an angry man. But no one has ever been able to frighten an angry woman. See. That is called an example. Now. Stop interrupting. Women must be made content through heart, through emotion. In this country of yours, that means by sex because women are not allowed to have any other emotions in this country, lest they put her name in the newspapers and everyone will point her out as a freak."

"Yeah, yeah, right, I've got it," said Remo who did not have any of it.

Then followed Chiun's thirty-seven steps toward bringing a woman sexual bliss. He cautioned Remo that these lessons were just as important as learning the correct method of the flutter stroke with the back of the knuckles.

Remo promised that he would practice Chiun's thirty-seven steps with great diligence and regularity, even as he did not practice the flutter stroke. But he found that when he had learned them, all thirty-seven, and was able to jellify women, he had lost almost all capacity for sexual pleasure. When he should be thinking about his own body, he was instead trying to remember if the next step was the woman's right knee or her left knee.

His training was also hindered by the fact that he had never gone past step eleven with any woman before jumping right ahead to step thirty-seven. He doubted that there was a woman in the world who could cope with steps twelve through thirty-six and keep her sanity, and when he asked Chiun about this, Chiun said that all thirty-seven steps were practiced regularly upon Korean

112

women, and Remo did not feel inclined to make such a sacrifice just to perfect his technique.

Maria Gonzales had taken off her short skirt and panties and was lying back on the bed. The skin of her body was as smooth and creamy as the skin of her face and Remo decided that whatever Maria Gonzales might be—spy, killer, revolutionary, agronomist, or left-wing twit—she looked like something more than just another assignment.

Remo moved alongside her in bed and quickly went through steps one, two, and three, which were merely to put her in the mood. Step four was the small of the back.

"Who's behind all these killings?" asked Remo.

"I do not know. What is the secret of Wondergrain?"

Step five was the inside of the left knee, followed by the right knee, and steps six and seven the perimeter of Maria's armpits.

"Why all this violence at Fielding's demonstration? Who hired the people to do it?"

"I do not know," said Maria. "How long have you known Fielding and what do you know about him?"

Step eight was the inside of the upper right thigh and step nine, the upper left thigh, closer to the heart.

"What can you tell me about what is going on?" asked Remo.

"Nothing," said Maria through tightly pressed lips. The word came out as a gasp. This time she did not ask a question.

Step ten was the mountain climbing of the fingers over the right breast. Maria's breath turned into sips of air. Her eyes which had watched Remo cagily now closed as her discipline weakened and she surrendered.

Good, Remo thought. She had held out a long time.

This time for sure. He'd get to step thirteen at least. The eleventh step was the slow trailing of fingers over the left breast to a peak which was hard and vibrant. Remo smiled. The twelfth step was next. He removed his hand from Maria's left breast. He began to move it down her body and Maria jumped into the air and clambered atop Remo, enveloping him, swallowing him up. Above him, her eyes flashed brilliant black and her lips bared her teeth in an involuntary rictus.

"To the lengths!" she screamed. "For Fidel!"

"To the lengths," Remo agreed dully. As she lowered her face to his neck to nip at it with her teeth, he shook his head slightly. That damn step eleven again. Someday he would. Someday, step twelve.

Maybe he was doing it wrong. He would have to ask Chiun. But there was no time to think about that now because he was deep, deep into step thirty-seven and he stayed in step thirty-seven a long time, much longer than Maria had ever been in step thirty-seven before and when that step was done, Maria collapsed off him and lay on her back staring at the ceiling, her eyes unfocused, almost glazed over.

"You didn't have anything to do with the killings?" Remo asked.

"No," she hissed. "I am a failure."

"Why?"

"Because I went to the lengths and you have not told me what I wanted to know."

"That's because I don't know anything," said Remo.

"Do not make sport of Maria, American. You are the keeper of the Constitution."

"Really, I don't know anything. If I knew anything, I would tell you."

114

"Several people who are the breakers of commodities . . . ."

"Brokers," Remo said.

"Yes. Brokers and contractors have been killed with Fielding. You know nothing of this?"

"Nothing. I thought you did." Something nagged at Remo. He remembered. Dead contractors. Jordan had mentioned that too before Remo had killed him but Jordan had not explained the contractors. Why contractors?

"Contractors?" he asked Maria. "What contractors?"

"Our intelligence people do not know. They think it may have something to do with Fielding's warehouse in Denver. I must see. I cannot fail my country."

"Don't be upset. There's always room for another Maria Gonzales in this hotel."

"I do not belong in this hotel. I am here to get the secrets of Wondergrain for my government."

"And if you fail, so what? I know Fielding. He's going to sell it so cheap it'll be like giving it away. Why pay for what's going to be a gift?"

"You do not understand socialist dedication," said Maria. She looked at him carefully. "Or capitalist greed."

"Maybe not." Remo was interrupted by a knock on the door. He rose lightly and went to the door, opened it and peered through the crack.

A man said, "I want to see Maria."

"You know Maria?" asked Remo.

"Yes. I was here last week."

"Wrong Maria," Remo said.

"I want to see Maria. I came up here to see Maria.

I want to see Maria. I won't wait to see Maria. I have to see Maria now."

"Go away," said Remo.

The man stamped his foot. "I won't go away. I want to see Maria. You've got no right to make me stop seeing Maria. Who are you anyway? Let me see Maria and when we're done, we'll have bacon, lettuce, and tomato sandwiches. On toast. I want a sandwich. With mayonnaise. On light toast. Whole wheat toast. They have good whole wheat toast across the street at Wimple's. I want to go to Wimple's. I have to have a sandwich. Why won't you let me go and have a sandwich? I'm going to Wimple's now and if they're all out of whole wheat toast, it'll be your fault for keeping me here talking. I'm hungry."

"What about Maria?" Remo asked.

"Maria? Who's Maria?" asked the man and walked away down the hall, a walk that wasn't quite a walk but more of a cross between it and a bunny hop, the walk of a child who just knows there has to be a bathroom somewhere around and is determined not to wet his pants, because he'll find it. Remo waited a while before closing the door, lest Peter Rabbit change his mind and come skipping back. But when he heard the elevator door close at the end of the hall, he went back into the room.

"Who was it?" Maria asked.

"I don't know. It was either Chicken Little or Henny Penny."

"I do not know these people," said Maria. As Remo turned, he saw Maria was up out of bed and full dressed.

"Where are you going in such a hurry?" he asked.

116

"To Denver. To see what I can find. You have pumped me . . . is that the word?"

"Almost," Remo said.

"Anyway, you have pumped me and I have pumped you, and we have found out that neither of us knows anything and so I will go to the Fielding warehouse in Denver to find out what I can find out." She smiled. "You were very good. I enjoyed myself."

"I won't tell Fidel," Remo said.

But Maria did not hear him. She was out of the room and gone, and Remo watched the closed door for a moment before sighing heavily and dressing himself.

CHAPTER TEN

Seven secretaries did not know where James Orayo Fielding was. The eighth and ninth knew but would not tell. The tenth knew and told, particularly after Remo had said that if she did not tell him where Fielding was, he would not come back to her apartment that night and explain to her, at very close range, why his facial bones were so hard and why his eyes were so dark.

Fielding had a penthouse suite atop the Hotel Walden, which differed from the Hotel Needham in the presence of hot water and cleanliness and the absence of hot-and-cold-running occupants all named John Smith.

"Of course I remember you," said Fielding. "We had that talk out in the Mojave, after that unpleasant violence. You're a government man, aren't you?"

"I didn't say that," said Remo.

"You didn't have to. You've got that look of someone who has a mission. I've found in life that the only people who have that look are people who work for a tight structure like a government . . . or people who are dying."

"Maybe they're the same people," said Remo.

"Could be," said Fielding, walking back away from Remo and sitting himself again behind his desk. "But on the other hand . . . ."

Remo, who had no tolerance for philosophy, jumped in with "I think people are trying to kill you, Mr. Fielding."

Fielding looked at Remo with large open eyes, bland and blank. "It wouldn't surprise me. There's money to be made in food. Anywhere money is to be made, there's potential for trouble."

"That's my question," said Remo. "Why don't you just give away the formula for Wondergrain? Just publish it and let it go at that?"

"Sit down . . . Remo, you said? . . . sit down. There's one simple reason, Remo. The same greed that may have people trying to kill me. That's the same greed that stops me from giving away my secrets. Human nature, son. Give away something and people think it's valueless. Put a price tag on it—any price tag, no matter how small—and it becomes like gold. People just won't accept what's free. Another thing. I had to make a deal with Feldman, O'Connor and Jordan to publicize Wondergrain. Well, they took over the ownership of it from me. And they want a profit. I thought I explained all this to you. Didn't I?"

Remo ignored the question. "I understand you've got a Denver warehouse?"

Fielding looked up quickly and his eyes hooded over. "Yes," he said slowly. He seemed about to say more, then stopped.

Remo waited, then said, "Don't you think you should have security guards there?"

"That's a good thought. But guards cost money. And frankly, all I had, my personal fortune, it's all gone into Wondergrain. I wouldn't worry too much about it though." He smiled, the satisfied smile of a cat licking its face after an uncooperative meal.

"Why not?"

"It kind of guards itself," said Fielding. "Anyway, anybody in there wouldn't know what it was all about anyway."

Remo shrugged. "I think you ought to be protected too. There's been just too much violence at your plantings."

"Are you volunteering, lad?" asked Fielding.

"If I have to."

"We have an old saying, at least in the Army I was in: never volunteer." Fielding essayed a small smile. It was the smile of a man who didn't care, Remo thought. Was it possible that Fielding's only purpose in life was to get his Wondergrains to the world and to hell with everything else?

"You aren't afraid?" asked Remo.

Fielding picked up the digital calendar from his desk. It read three months, eleven days. "I have no more than that to live. You think I've got something to worry about? Just let me get my work done."

Later, talking to Chiun in their room, Remo said, "He's an incredible man, Little Father. All he wants to do is some good for mankind."

Chiun merely nodded. He had taken to becoming morose in the daytime hours lately since he had begun boycotting the television soap operas. Instead, he spent his time with pen and inkwell and large sheets of paper, writing letters to television stations, demanding that they stop introducing false violence into their daytime dramas or he would not be responsible for the consequences. He gave each of them three days in which to acknowledge the acceptance of his demand. The three days was up today.

Remo noticed Chiun's nod was unenthusiastic.

"All right, Little Father, something's wrong. What is it?"

"Since when have you become so interested in mankind?"

"I'm not."

"Then why are you so interested in this Fielding person?"

"Because even if I'm not interested in mankind, it's nice to meet someone who is. Little Father, he's a good man."

"And *As the Planet Revolves* was a good story. Good and true. But it isn't anymore."

"Meaning?"

"One spells out small words only for children." And Chiun folded his arms and stubbornly refused to explain his remark.

"Do you know why organizations should never promote people?" asked Remo.

"No. But I am sure you will tell me."

"Now that you're a coequal partner, you've stopped working. It happens all the time."

Chiun snorted.

"All right," Remo said. "You sit there, but I'm going to make sure that no one rips off Fielding's formula. If he wants to give it away on his own terms, well, then I'm going to make those terms work."

"Waste your time anyway you wish. Since you picked

121

this assignment, I will sit here thinking of something important to do on our next assignment. Since I am a coequal partner now, I have the right to choose."

"Do what you want." Remo went into the next room and flopped onto the bed. First things first. He was dealing now with two threats: some force that was using violence and might have Fielding as its target, and Maria Gonzales who was trying to steal Fielding's formula.

He dialed the Hotel Needham and recognized the oily desk clerk.

"Remember me?" Remo said. "I came by to see Maria Gonzales, the Cuban one, the other day."

"Yes sir, I certainly do," said the clerk.

"Is Maria back?"

"No."

"There's another fifty in it for you if you let me know when she comes back to her room."

"As soon as," the clerk said.

"Good. Don't forget," said Remo, and gave the clerk his number, then closed his eyes and slept.

But when the phone rang, it was not the clerk. It was the lemony whine of Dr. Harold Smith.

"I wouldn't like to hang by my thumbs waiting for you to report."

"That's funny. That's just what I'd like you to do," said Remo.

"There were three persons . . . er, found at that planting site in Ohio. Any of that yours?"

"All three of them." Quickly Remo filled in Smith on what had happened and what he had learned. "I don't know why," he said, "but it seems someone's gunning for Fielding."

122

"It could be. I'll leave that with you. It's not why I called."

"Why did you call? Am I overdrawn on expenses again this month?"

"We have some early indications that someone—we can't say who yet—is trying to get close to us. Questions are being asked around. Anyone close to us might be getting close to you."

"That'd be their tough luck."

"Maybe yours too," said Smith. "Be careful."

"Your concern is deeply appreciated."

CHAPTER ELEVEN

Maria did not return until the next day, but she would not have had time to take off her hat before the room clerk at the Hotel Needham called Remo.

"Hey, pal, this is your old friend at the Hotel Needham."

"She's back?"

"Just got in." He paused. "Your turn now," he added with a dirty-minded chuckle.

"Thanks," said Remo who did not feel thanks and determined then to beat the clerk out of the fifty he had promised him.

Maria was a long time answering Remo's knocking at the door and when she did her face was drawn and pallid.

"Oh, it's you," she said. "Well, as long as you are here, come in. But don't ask me to go the lengths."

"What's wrong? You look awful."

"I feel awful," said Maria. She wore an identical outfit to the one she had worn two days before. She

124

locked the door behind Remo and then sat down heavily on the chair at the small Formica-topped desk the Hotel Needham provided, apparently for that .0001 percent of people who paid by check. She tried a thin smile. "Must be Montezuma's revenge. I have the upthrows."

Remo sat on the edge of the bed facing her.

"So what did you find out?"

"And why should I tell you? We are on different sides."

"No, we're not. We both want Fielding's formulas to get to the world. If you can steal them for your country, fine," Remo lied. "I'm only worried about keeping him alive so that everyone isn't cheated out of them."

Maria did not speak as she thought about this for a while. "All right," she said finally. "Anyway, it is not like I am giving away anything. You are the keeper of the Constitution. If I do not cooperate, you may have me deported from your country. Or worse. Is that not right?"

"That's it exactly," said Remo. If justification was what she wanted, justification was what she'd get. "I'd go to any lengths to find out what you learned."

Maria raised a right index finger in warning. "I told you. No 'to the lengths'." Remo noticed the tip of her finger was discolored and blistered.

"So what did you find?"

"I found Mr. Fielding's warehouse. It is not in Denver however. It is outside Denver. It is in a big building that is carved into the side of a rocky hill outside the city."

"And what was there?"

"Nothing. Barrels of grain. And barrels of a liquid

I could not identify." She held up her finger again. "Whatever it was, it was powerful. It did this to me." She looked ruefully at the blister, seemed about to speak, then jumped to her feet and ran for the bathroom. Remo could hear her retching, and then the toilet being flushed. Maria returned, her face even whiter than before.

"Forgive me."

"No workers there? No guards. Nobody?"

"There was no one to be seen. Just barrels and that was all." Her voice trailed off as she spoke and she seemed ready to pass out. Remo got up and went to her side.

"Listen, Maria. You've got probably a touch of flu or virus or something."

"A virus," she said. "Americans always have the virus."

"Right," Remo said. "A virus. Anyway, you shouldn't stay here alone until you're well. I want you to come with me."

"Aha. A Yankee plot. Get Maria away from her room and then throw her in a dungeon."

"We don't have dungeons. Except in New York, and there they call them apartments."

"All right. A jail cell."

"No. Just a clean hotel room where you can get some rest."

"Alone? With you? That is not moral."

Remo thought this strange for a girl who forty-eight hours before had gone to the lengths, but he shook his head. "No. We'll have a chaperone. Chiun."

"The gracious Oriental?"

"I think so."

"Good. Then I will go. He is a man of much wisdom and kindness and he will protect me from you."

In the lobby, Remo sat Maria in the only chair that might have won even conditional approval from the city's building department and approached the oily clerk.

"I owe you something," said Remo.

"Well, don't look on it as owing. I did a favor. You're going to do me a favor."

Remo nodded. "Fifty favors if I remember right."

"You remember right."

Remo leaned on the desk casually. On a table behind it he saw a small cashbox.

"Want to play double or nothing?" Remo asked.

The clerk's eyes narrowed warily. "Actually, no."

Remo reached into his pocket and pulled out a fifty. He held it away from his body in his right hand. "It'd be easy," he said. He manipulated his fingers, almost as if playing an imaginary piano with a vertical keyboard, and the bill vanished. "Just tell me what hand it's in," he said nodding toward his right fist.

"That's all?" said the clerk, glancing quickly at Remo's left hand, resting on the counter, four feet away from the fifty. "That's all?" he repeated.

"That's all."

"Double or nothing?" said the clerk.

"Double or nothing. What hand's it in?"

"That one," said the clerk with a sheepish smile, pointing to Remo's right hand.

"Look and see," said Remo. He extended his right hand toward the clerk. As he did, his left hand was over the counter, opening the cashbox and flipping through the bills there. With his fingertips, he felt for the twenties and peeled off eight, curled them into a tube, closed the box, and put the $160 into his left pants pocket. Meanwhile, the clerk was trying to pry open Remo's right hand.

"How can I tell if I won?" he asked plaintively.

Remo relaxed his fingers and opened his hand. Curled up in the palm was the fifty-dollar bill.

The clerk grinned and snatched up the bill. "Terrific," he said. "Now you owe me another fifty."

"You're right," said Remo. He dug into his right-hand pocket but brought his hand out empty. From his left pocket, he pulled out the tube of twenties.

He unrolled them and counted off three. "I'm out of fifties. Here. You've been such a good guy. Take sixty." He handed the bills to the clerk who set them on top of the fifty and quickly jammed them all into his pocket.

"Thanks, old buddy."

"Anytime," said Remo. He walked away, the hotel's other five twenties in his pocket, offsetting the two fifties of his own he had given away. He whistled as he escorted Maria from the building.

She felt worse when Remo reached his hotel and he quickly put her into bed. Chiun was sitting in the middle of the living room floor when they entered but he did not speak, not even to acknowledge their greetings. When Maria was sleeping, Remo came back outside.

"You're a real charmer when you want to be, Chiun."

"I am not paid to be charming."

"Good thing."

"Remo, how could they do it? How could they do violence to the beautiful daytime dramas? I have sat here this night and asked myself that and I do not know the answer."

"It was probably a mistake, Little Father. Start watching again. You'll see. It was probably just a thing they did once and won't do again."

"You really think so?"

"Sure," said Remo, feeling very unsure.

"We will see," said Chiun. "I will hold you personally responsisble for this."

"Hold on, hold on, hold on. I'm not in charge of the television shows. Blame somebody else."

"Yes. But you are an American. You should know what goes on in the minds of the other meat-eaters. If not you, who?"

Remo sighed. He looked in on Maria who was sleeping deeply then went into the living room to sleep on the couch. Chiun meanwhile had unrolled his sleeping mat in the middle of the floor and, reassured by what he would forever regard as Remo's personal word that the daytime dramas would not again be sullied by violence, had fallen instantly asleep. For five seconds of sleep, he seemed like a normal man, breathing normally; for the next ten seconds he was the Master of Sinanju, breathing deeply and almost silently; and then he turned into a flock of geese.

"Honnnnk," he snored on the intake. "Hnnnnnnk," he snored on the exhaust.

Remo sat up on the couch. He was about to make the decision, one he had made often before, that sleep this night would be impossible, when the telephone rang.

Chiun's snoring stopped abruptly but he slept on. Remo was at the phone halfway during the first ring. He picked it up.

"Hello."

He was answered with the click of someone hanging up.

Remo shrugged, and went back to the couch. Wrong number probably. If a man answers, hang up. At least the phone had stopped the snoring.

He lay back down on the couch.

"Hooonnnnnnk." Intake.

"Hooonnnnnnk." Exhaust.

"Shit." Remo.

He left the suite, went downstairs out into the early morning air of Dayton, filled his lungs deeply, and immediately wished he hadn't. There were trace elements of arsenic, carbon monoxide, sulphur dioxide, cyannic gas, hydrochloric acid, swamp gas, and methane.

And then he forgot the air as he sensed something else, an unconscious pressure on him as if he were living inside a dark, opaque balloon and a giant was squeezing the sides. He stopped for a moment, not breathing, not moving, just sensing and knew he felt it.

He turned toward the left, began to step in that direction, then wheeled and came back toward the right. Behind him, he heard a soft spat, a click, and a thud.

He did not turn to see what it was. It was a bullet. The pressure had been a marksman zeroing in on him. From the way the bullet had hit behind him, smacking the hotel wall then a water outlet pipe and then the sidewalk, Remo judged it came from the roof of a building across the street.

That was the phone call. To try to get him outside.

Remo moved along the sidewalk, apparently walking casually. To a passerby, he would seem to be another insomniac out for an aimless early morning stroll. But to Anthony Polski, atop the roof of an old apartment building across the street, Remo seemed to be moving like a squirrel. A burst forward, a pause, a burst, a pause. It was as if Remo were in darkness and was illuminated only by the flashing of a strobe light at random intervals.

Polski sighted down the barrel of his silencer-equipped rifle, peering carefully through the light-gathering scope. There he was. Moving ahead slowly. He led Remo just a hair with the rifle, then softly squeezed the trigger. But even as he squeezed and the rifle softly fired, he knew he had missed. In the scope he saw Remo stop, pause, then start again at a slightly different angle.

The bullet splatted almost quietly against a wall ahead of Remo. Angry now, Polski fired again, allowing for Remo's pause, allowing for his stopping, leading him, but then stopping the lead and shooting right at where Remo stood. When he fired, he knew he had missed again. The bullet hit into the wall behind Remo.

On the street, Remo had learned enough. Only one marksman up there. If there had been more, shots would have bracketed him by now. He moved into a doorway. Across the street, Polski saw him move into the doorway. He circled the edges of the doorway with a slight movement of the tip of his rifle barrel. Sooner or later, the bastard'd have to come out of that doorway and it wouldn't be any stop-and-go movement then. He would have to come straight out and when he did, Polski would let him have it right in the chest. He lay there, arms propped up on the slight roof overhang, the tip of the rifle moving back and forth gently, and waited.

"Pardon me, boy, is this the Pennsylvania Station? I'm the Minister of Silly Walks."

The voice came from behind Polski. He rolled onto his back, wheeling the gun around, pointing it at the other end of the roof. There he was. The bastard was standing there, thirty feet away, smiling.

"No. This is the morgue," said Polski grimly and he jerked down on the trigger of the rifle.

The shot missed. The bastard wasn't there. There he was, six feet off to the side and closing.

"Son of a bitch," Polski yelled and fired again. But he missed and Remo kept moving, sideways, frontwards, skittering crablike across the roof and Polski had but one more chance and even before he fired that shot, he knew, with a sickening thump deep into inside his stomach, that it would miss too.

Polski felt the rifle come loose from his hands and then *he* was standing there, smiling down at Polski, the rifle held loosely across his two hands. He had thick wrists, Polski saw.

Polski kicked up at the man standing above him, aiming a hard leather-clad toe toward the groin, but that missed too and Polski gave up and just lay there.

"Who sent you here, fella?" asked Remo.

"Nobody."

"Let's try again. Who sent you here?"

"Shoot and get it over with," said Polski.

"No such luck, junior," said Remo. Then Polski felt a pain in his shoulder, as if a shark had just bitten out a large chunk of it.

He wanted his shoulder back. "A contract. I got it by phone," he hissed, through pain-distorted lips.

"From who?"

"I don't know. It came on the phone and the money came by mail. I never saw nobody."

"Money? Tell me. What am I worth these days?"

"I got five thousand for you and they told me how to do it. From up here on the roof."

132

Remo squeezed, Polski pleaded, and Remo knew he was not lying. He released the shoulder. Polski cringed against the small brick wall atop the roof.

"What are you gonna do to me?"

"What would you do if you were me?"

"Yeah," said Polski. "But that was a contract. I didn't mean anything against you."

"Well, don't you go thinking that this means I don't like you," said Remo and then Polski saw a flash and then, not stars but one single bright star and then he felt nothing more, not himself being lifted up, not himself being dropped off the edge of the building, not himself getting tangled in the rope of the building's ancient metal flagpole. He came there to an abrupt stop, hanging off the flagpole like a pennant for a long-ago World Series.

Remo looked down on Polski. "That's the biz, sweetheart."

He put the rifle back onto the roof and trotted lightly toward the back of the building and the drainpipe he had clambered up.

Even though he had learned nothing, he felt good. A little exercise was good for both the body and spirit. And then he did not feel quite so good anymore. His senses told him Polski had not been alone. There was someone else.

Remo went over the edge of the roof and started down the drainpipe. The pipe was warm in places under his hands. The rough-painted cast iron did not draw the heat from his hands the way it should. As he went down, he felt the warmer spots on the pipe. The spread between them was sixteen inches. That meant a small man had climbed the pipe after Remo.

As he neared the ground, Remo glanced back up.

Against the dark shadow of the roof overhang was an area of slightly darker shadow and Remo forced the pupils of his eyes to open even wider, absorbing light from darkness, giving up the precise and narrow but light-robbing focus, and he was able to make out a head peering over the roof. It was wearing a black hood.

A black hood?

Ninja. The ancient Oriental art of deception, invisibility, hiding, and then attacking out of darkness.

At the end of the alley, the dark walls on both sides ended in a bright rectangle of light, illuminated by the street beyond.

Remo sensed movement to the left of him, in the shadows. He breathed deeply, then paused, saturating all his tissues with oxygen. He did it again. And then stopped breathing, so the sound of his breathing did not interfere with his senses. Behind him he heard the faint rustle of linen—the black linen night-fighting suit of the Ninja—and he knew it was the man coming down the drainpipe. It would probably be an attack from the rear. He took a step toward the front of the alley, slowly. There was a faint rustling to the right also. They had him boxed, left, right, and back. The exit from the alley, brightly lighted, might be a trap also. They could have men waiting there for him.

He kept strolling casually toward the light at the end of the alley, and then, casually still, without seeming to change stride or direction, he melted into the shadows along the right side of the wall. There, in pitch blackness, he paused. He heard breathing near him. He worked his eyes again, and saw an Oriental man in a full black costume. He had not yet seen Remo, although they were close enough to kiss. Remo reached out his right hand and grabbed the man's thin neck through the linen.

He touched the exact spot with the exact amount of pressure required. The man neither moved nor made a sound. Remo held on and waited. He heard the rustle of footsteps moving down the alley, following the path he had taken. Then all sounds stopped. Their quarry had disappeared. Where had he gone?

And then the small man at the end of Remo's right hand went flying out into the alley and hit the man who had come down from the roof, in the midsection. The second man crumbled with a noisy "ooooof."

Remo was out of the darkness and into the parallelogram of light, silhouetted against the brightness of the street beyond.

The first Ninja man was finished; he would never again skulk down an alley. The second scrambled to his feet, unaccustomed to the bright flash of light that shone in his eyes over Remo's shoulder as Remo moved out of the light.

Remo took him out with an index finger to the right temple, and then decided he should have used a back elbow thrust. He did and was rewarded with a satisfying bone-crushing crunch.

Chiun should have been there to see that, he thought, but then he thought no more as he moved into the shadows on the left where one more was hiding, and he stopped, and cut off his breathing, and he heard the tiny sip of air characteristic of Ninja, as if the man were breathing through a straw, and Remo followed the sound and was on him.

But the man darted away, slipping into the darkness, and across the silence and the blackness the two men faced each other as if it were high noon in Dodge City.

The Ninja waited, as was traditional, for Remo to make a move, a mistake that would open him to the Ninja's counterthrust, but Remo made a move that was no mistake and the back of his left foot was deep into the muscle and gut of the man's stomach.

As the man fell, he gasped: "Who are you?"

"Sinanju, buddy. The real thing," Remo said.

Remo left the bodies behind and walked out onto the sidewalk. He looked upward over his right shoulder, toward the roof, where Anthony Polski dangled by his neck from the flagpole and Remo threw him a snappy military salute.

He paused again and behind him he heard a faint sound . . . a tiny repetitive clicking . . . but he sensed it as machinery and not a weapon and he decided to ignore it and go back to his room. Perhaps now, having exercised, he could sleep.

Above the alley, on the roof of another nearby building, Emil Growling quickly packed away his camera loaded with infrared motion picture film and headed home for a long night's work in his darkroom.

Not that he minded. He was being paid a great deal of money to have those films processed by morning. And later when he saw the films, he would realize he might have been witness to something special. Even though he had barely been able to see what was happening while it was happening because of the darkness, the films were sharp, almost seeming brightly lighted, and as he watched the thin white man with the thick wrists move, he was glad that the infinitesimal clicking of his motion picture camera had not given him away.

CHAPTER TWELVE

Refreshed and invigorated by the night's exercise he had given his adenoids, Chiun was awake before Remo.

Remo found him sitting in the middle of the floor, right hand pressed up against the right side of his nose, breathing in through one nostril and exhaling through the other.

"You look in?" said Remo. "How's the girl?"

"Dead," said Chiun without interrupting his exercise.

Remo sat up on the couch. "Dead? How?"

"She died in the night. After you went out and left me here all alone, I lay here listening to her breathe and one moment she was there and there was the breath of life and the next moment there was no breath and she was dead."

"Didn't you try to help her?"

"That is unkind," said Chiun, lowering his right hand from his nose. "She was a very nice lady and I tried to help her. But she was beyond help. This is a very bad thing."

"When did you start worrying about bodies?" asked Remo.

He got up and walked past Chiun into the bedroom. Maria Gonzales lay peaceful in death, covers pulled up tightly to her neck.

Remo stood alongside the girl, looking down at her body. Her right hand rested on the pillow next to her head and the blister on the tip of her index finger seemed larger than it had the day before. Remo pulled down the sheet. Maria's body made him shake his head. Yesterday so white and creamy it had seemed like freshly stirred wall paint, it was now covered with red and yellow oozing blisters that seemed to weep like rheumy tired old eyes.

Remo grimaced, then pulled the sheet back up. When he turned away, Chiun stood in the door.

"I've never seen anything like that, Little Father," said Remo.

"It is not chemicals or poison," said Chiun. "It is something else."

"Yeah. But what?"

"I have seen it before," said Chiun. "Many years ago, in Japan. After the big bomb."

Radiation blisters.

In the living room, Remo's first phone call was to Dr. Smith. He told him about Maria's body and told him to make arrangements to have the body collected and an autopsy run upon it.

"Why?" asked Smith. "Isn't it just another of your usual bodies? Necks broken, skulls crushed, dismemberment. I've been reading the paper. People hanging from flagpoles."

"No," said Remo. "I think it's radiation poisoning and I think you better tell the people who collect it to be careful."

He started to hang up, then added, "And unless you want another missile crisis, you'd better find some neat way of disposing of the body and just let Cuba think their spy was lost."

"Thank you for your advice, Remo. Have you ever considered . . . ."

Before Smith could finish the sentence, Remo had depressed the receiver button and was dialing his second call.

No, Mr. Fielding was not in his office. He was out inspecting the four Wondergrain sites around America. Of course, the secretary remembered Remo. She was angry with him for not coming to her apartment as he had promised, but not so angry that she would withdraw the invitation forever. Yes, she understood about business. Some time soon. Yes. And oh yes, Mr. Fielding went to the Mojave site first. He had left only this morning. Now about Remo's brown eyes . . . .

Remo hung up, satisfaction jousting with dissatisfaction. He was satisfied that Fielding was still alive. Whoever had been behind last night's attacks on Remo had not reached Fielding yet. But Remo was dissatisfied with Fielding's security. That dizzo secretary had been quick enough to tell Remo where Fielding was. She might tell anybody just as quickly.

Because they were now coequal partners, Remo asked Chiun if he wanted to accompany Remo to the Mojave.

"No," said Chiun. "You go."

"Why?"

"If you have seen one desert, you have seen them

139

all. I have seen the Sahara. What do I need with your Mojave? Besides, I am going to take your advice and watch my beautiful stories today. I believe your promise that there will be no more violence to mar them."

"Hold on, Little Father, it's not my promise."

"Do not try to go back on your word now. I remember what you said, as if it were just a moment ago. You personally guaranteed that there would be no more violence. I am holding you to that promise."

Remo sighed softly. What it meant was that Chiun had weakened and was going back to his television shows and nothing Remo could say or do would stop him. But if the shows went badly, Chiun wanted someone to blame.

After arranging for Chiun, his trunks, and his television set to be quietly shipped to a new hotel, Remo went to the Vandalia Airport. A quick jet flight and a helicopter ride brought him to the edge of the Mojave and a rented Yamaha motorcycle brought him out into the desert.

Mile after mile, following the narrow road, as straight as a weighted string hanging inside a well, Remo rode on into the heat and sand. Far ahead, on the rise off to the left, he saw the hurricane fencing surrounding Fielding's experimental farm, and he saw tire tracks through the sand.

He ran ahead another mile, then made a sharp left off the road and dug his bike twistingly through the sand, sputtering and spitting, following the other tire tracks, until he reached the fence.

A uniformed guard surveyed him from inside the fence.

"I'm Remo Barker. I work for Mr. Fielding. Where

is he?" Remo could see a small pickup truck with rental plates parked inside the compound.

"He's over inspecting the field," the guard said lazily. He unlocked the wire gate by pressing a button built into a panel on an inside post.

Remo propped up the motorcycle and walked inside. "Must be kind of lonely duty out here," he said.

"Yeah," said the guard. "Sometimes." He nodded toward the small wooden shack inside the compound. "Me and two other fellows around the clock." He leaned over to Remo and said softly, "Strange. Who'd want to steal wheat?"

"That's what I keep asking myself," Remo said walking toward the area in the back, covered by the almost-black plastic sun shield. The compound itself was almost a hundred yards square. The planting field took up one-quarter of the space. The only other thing inside the hurricane fencing was the guard's small wooden shack.

There was no sign of Fielding. Remo went to the edge of the planting area, then lifted up a corner of the plastic sun shield and stepped inside.

It was a miracle.

Thrusting up from the arid, barren sand of the Mojave was a field of young wheat. To the left was rice. In the back, barley and soybeans. And there was that strange smell Remo remembered from the first time he had been there. He recognized it now. It was oil.

He looked around, but could not see Fielding. He walked through the field, through a miracle of growth, expecting to find Fielding crouched down, inspecting some stalk of grain, but there was no sign of the man.

At the back of the planting area, Remo lifted an edge of the sunscreen to find that it had been erected right

141

against the hurricane fencing. There was no place for Fielding to be. He looked between the sunscreen and the fencing, left and right, toward the angled corners of the hurricane fencing but saw nothing, not even a lizard.

Where could Fielding have vanished to? Then he heard a truck's motor start and tires begin to drive off through the heavy sand.

Remo went back through the planting area, stuffing samples of the grains in his pockets. At the gate, he saw the truck speeding off in the distance.

"That Fielding?"

"Yeah," said the guard.

"Where'd he come from?"

The guard shrugged. "I told him you was here but he said he was in a hurry and had a plane to catch."

Remo walked out through the gate, hopped on his Yamaha, and took off through the sand after Fielding.

Fielding was driving along the narrow road at seventy miles an hour and it took Remo almost two miles to catch up to him. He pulled up alongside Fielding's open window and then thought himself stupid for startling the man, because Fielding jerked the wheel and the truck spun left and sideswiped Remo's motorcycle.

The cycle started to lean to its side and Remo threw his weight heavily in the other direction and pulled back on the bike, but the front wheel lifted as Remo regained its balance, and the motorcycle did a fast wheelie, standing up on its end, while Remo guided it through the deep sand to a safe stop off the road.

Fielding had stopped on the road and looked out the window, back at Remo.

"Hey, you startled me. You could've been hurt," he said.

"No sweat," said Remo. He looked at the dented bike and said "I'll ride in with you if you don't mind."

"No. Come on. You drive."

Driving back toward the airport, Remo said, "Some disappearing act back there. Where were you?"

"Back at the farm? In the field."

"I didn't see you."

"I must have come out just as you were going in. It's coming like a charm, isn't it? Is that what you came for, to see how my crops are doing?"

"No. I came to tell you I think your life is in danger."

"Why? Who would care about me?"

"I don't know," said Remo. "But there's just too much violence about this whole thing."

Fielding shook his head slowly. "It's too late now for anybody to do anything. The crops are coming so good that I'm moving up the schedule. Three more days and I'm going to show them to the world. The miracle grains. Humanity's salvation. I thought they'd take a month to grow, but they didn't even take two weeks."

He looked at Remo and smiled. "And then I'll be done."

Fielding would not hear of Remo accompanying him to the other planting fields.

"Look," he said. "You're talking about violence but all the violence seems aimed at you. None at me. Maybe you're a target, not me."

"I doubt it," said Remo. "There's another thing too. A girl went to your Denver warehouse." He felt Fielding stiffen on the seat. "She died. Radiation poisoning."

"Who was she?" Fielding asked.

"A Cuban, trying to steal your formulas."

"That's a shame. It's dangerous in Denver." He

looked at Remo hard. "Can I trust you? I'll tell you something no one else knows. It's a special kind of radiation that prepared the grain so it can give such miracle growth. It's dangerous if you don't know what you're doing. I feel sorry for the poor girl." He shook his head. "I haven't felt this bad since my manservant, Oliver, was killed in a tragic accident. Would you like to see his picture?"

In the mirror, Remo saw Fielding's lips pull back in a grimace. Or was it a grin? Never mind. Many people smiled when under tension.

"No, I'll skip the pictures," Remo said. As he parked the truck at the airport later, Fielding put a hand on his arm. "Look. Maybe you're right. Maybe these attacks are eventually aimed at me. But if they think the way to me is through you, then it's best we're separated. You see my point?"

Reluctantly Remo nodded. It was logical, but it made him uneasy. For once, he had found a job he wanted to do. Maybe in decades or generations, if Remo's life ever became known, maybe he would not be rated by the people he had killed but for this one life he had saved—the life of James Orayo Fielding, the man who had conquered hunger and starvation and famine in the world for all time.

He thought this while he watched Fielding's plane take off. He thought of it on his own plane back to Dayton and he thought of it when, just on a whim, he remembered his pockets filled with grain and stopped at an agricultural lab at the University of Ohio.

"Perfectly good grain," the botanist told Remo. "Normal, healthy specimens, of wheat, barley, soy, and rice."

"And what would you say if I told you they were grown in the Mojave Desert?"

The botanist smiled, showing a set of teeth that were discolored by tobacco stains.

"I'd say you'd been spending too much time in the sun without a hat."

"They were," said Remo.

"No way."

"You've heard of it," Remo said. "Fielding's Wondergrains. This is it."

"I've heard of it, sure. But that doesn't mean I have to believe it. Look, friend, there's one miracle nobody can do. Rice cannot be grown in anything but mud. Mud. That's dirt and water. Mud, pal."

"In this process, the plants draw their moisture from the air," Remo said patiently.

The botanist laughed, too loud and too long.

"In the Mojave? There is no moisture in the air in the Mojave. Humidity zero. Try drawing moisture out of that air." And he was off laughing again.

Remo stuffed his samples back into his pockets. "Remember," he said. "They laughed at Luther Burbank when he invented the peanut. They laughed at all the great men."

The botanist was obviously one of those who would have laughed at Luther Burbank because he was giggling when Remo left. "Rice. In the desert. Peanuts. Luther Burbank. Hahahahahaha."

CHAPTER THIRTEEN

With the ratchety click of a child's toy, the small 16mm movie projector whirred into fan movement, flashed light, and fired a string of pictures on the beaded glass screen in front of Johnny "Deuce" Deussio.

"Hey, Johnny, how many times you gonna look at this guy? I tell you, you just give me three good guys. No fancy stuff. We just go and pop him."

"Shut up, Sally," said Deussio. "In the first place, you couldn't find three good guys. And if you did, you wouldn't know what to do with them."

Sally grunted, his feelings hurt, his hatred for this skinny, bone-faced motion picture subject growing by the second.

"Anyway," he grumbled, "if I had a chance at him, he wouldn't be throwing no people off no roof."

"You had your chance at him, Sally," said Deussio. "The night he sneaked in here. Right past you. Right past all your guards. And he stuffed my head in a toilet."

"That was him?"

Sally looked at the screen again with greater interest. He watched as Remo seemed to stroll casually down a street, while bullets pinged around him. "He don't look like much."

"You dumb shit," Deussio yelled. "What do you think *you* would do if somebody was on a roof across the street, popping away at you with a rifle and a night scope?"

"I'd run, Johnny. I'd run."

"That's right. You'd run. And the shooter would give you a lead and then put a bullet right in your brain. If he could find one. And this guy that you don't think is much made that goddamn shooter miss just by walking away. Now you get your stupid ass out of here and let me figure out how."

After Sally left, Johnny Duece settled back in his chair and watched the film again. He watched as Remo climbed a drainpipe as effortlessly as if it were a ladder. He watched as he made the marksman miss up close and then threw him off the roof into the flagpole rope.

He watched Remo come back down the drainpipe and watched Remo pause on the pipe, feeling it with his fingertips, and he knew that at that moment Remo had sensed that someone else had followed him up the pipe.

But Remo had continued down and Johnny Deuce watched the movie and watched his own man come back down and he watched three of them stake out Remo in the alley and the three of them wind up dead.

The last shot was of Remo standing in the light at the opening of the alley, looking upward at the marksman's body twisting slowly, slowly in the wind, and tossed a salute.

Deussio hit the rewind button and the film started clicking back to the load reel. As he sat in the darkness, Deussio knew there was something in the film, something he should be able to figure out.

He had sent a modern attack—an armed rifleman—against this Remo and he had sent an Eastern-style attack, three Ninja warriors. Remo had wiped them all out. How?

Johnny Deuce pressed the forward button again. The projector lamp lit and the screen filled with the black and white images. Deussio watched Remo, seeming to walk casually, dodging sniper's bullets. Deussio had seen a walk like that before.

He watched the film as Remo climbed the drainpipe easily. Deussio had seen climbing like that before.

He saw Remo dodge bullets on the rooftop. He had been told before of people who could do that.

He stopped the projector to think.

Where before?

Where?

Right. Ninja. The Ninja techniques of the Oriental night-fighters involved things like that—the walk, the climbing, the bullet dodging.

OK. So Remo was a Ninja. But then why didn't the three Ninja men get to him? Three should have been better than one.

Johnny Deuce pressed the button again. The projector whirred and the pictures flashed. He sat up straighter as he saw his three Ninja men surround Remo, in perfect positions, and then all wind up lumps of deadness.

Why?

He stopped the projector again. He sat and thought.

He ran the film to the end. He rewound it. He showed it again. And again. And again. And he thought.

And finally, just before midnight, Johnny Deuce jumped out of his chair, clapping his hands together, whooping in joy.

Sally came into the room on the dead run, automatic in hand. He saw Deussio alone in the middle of the floor smiling.

"What's wrong, boss? What happened?

"Nothing. I figured it out. I figured it out."

"Figured what out, boss?"

Johnny Deuce looked at Sally for a moment. He didn't want to tell him, but he had to tell somebody and even though the brilliance of it would all be lost on Sally, it was better than keeping it inside himself.

"He mixes his techniques. Against a Western-style attack, he uses an Eastern defense. Against an Eastern attack, he uses a Western defense. When our Ninja guys went after him, he didn't do any fancy moves. He just dove into them like a goddamn machine and piled up the bodies. Rip. Slash. He had them. That's the secret. He defends in the way opposite to the attack."

"Dat's terrific, boss," said Sally who had no idea of what Johnny Deuce was talking about.

"I knew you'd appreciate it," said Deussio. "Well, I know you can appreciate this. He gave us the key for going after him. The way to get him."

"Yeah?" said Sally, paying more attention now. These were things he understood. "How?"

"Simultaneous attacks. Eastern and Western style at once. He can't use just one style to defense them. If he goes East defense, the East attack'll get him. If he

149

goes West defense, the West attack'll get him." Johnny Deuce clapped his hands again. "Beautiful. Just goddamn beautiful."

"Sure is, boss," said Sally who had again gotten lost.

"You don't know, Sally. Because, we get this guy out of the way and we move in on Force X."

"Force X?" Sally was getting more and more out of it.

"Yes."

"Well, okay, boss, but listen. You want me to get some guys from the east and the west to go after this lug? Back east, there's a terrific pair of brothers. They say they're great with chains. And for the western attack, I got these two friends of mine in LA and . . . ."

Sally had been smiling. He stopped when he saw the cloud come over Deussio's face.

"Get out of here, you stupid shit," said Deussio and dismissed Sally with a wave of his hand.

It wasn't worth it. How could he explain Force X to Sally who thought a Western attack meant one from Los Angeles and an Eastern attack meant New York City?

How tell him about the computer printouts, gathering all the information on arrests and convictions and crooked politicians bagged, and how the computers had confirmed the existence of a counterforce to crime and had high-probability located it in the northeast in Rye, New York. High probability, Folcroft Sanitarium.

It all waited for him now, wiping out Force X. But first this Remo would have to go. First him.

Deussio went to his desk, took out paper and pencil and from the bottom right-hand drawer a pocket calculator, and he set to work. There was no margin for error.

Well, that was all right. Johnny Deuce didn't make errors.

He told himself that more than once. But it didn't help. There was something in the back of his mind and it was telling him he had forgotten something or someone. But, for the life of him, he couldn't think of what it was.

Not for the life of him.

CHAPTER FOURTEEN

"I don't understand it, Little Father."

"It belongs then in a vast category of human knowledge," said Chiun. "Which of the many things you do not understand are you talking about?"

"I don't understand this about Fielding. If someone wants to attack him, why have they been coming at us first? Why not go right after him? That's Mystery Number One."

Chiun waved his left hand as if it were beneath him even to think of Mystery Number One.

Remo waited for an answer but got none. Chiun sat instead in his saffron robe on a tufted pillow in the middle of the floor and gave Remo his fullest attention. It was Sunday and Chiun's soap operas had not been on the television that or the previous day, although he had watched them for the preceding two days and satisfied himself that Remo had fulfilled his promise to keep violence off the TV screen.

"And then there's Mystery Number Two. Maria died

152

from radioactive poisoning. Smith's autopsy showed that. Fielding has a radioactive warehouse. But the grain samples I brought back show no signs of radioactivity. How can that be? That's Mystery Number Two."

With a wave of his right hand, Chiun consigned Mystery Number Two to the same scrap heap as Mystery Number One.

"How did Fielding disappear in the desert when I was looking for him?" started Remo.

"Wait," said Chiun. "Is this Mystery Number Three?"

"Yes," said Remo.

"All right. You may proceed. I just want to be sure to keep them all straight."

"Mystery Number Three," said Remo. "Fielding disappears in the desert. Where was he? Was he lying when he said he must have just come out from under the sun-filter just as I was going in? I think he was lying. Why would he lie when he knows I'm trying to protect him?"

Pffft with both hands. So much for Mystery Number Three.

"Why so many deaths surrounding this project, for God's sake? Commodities men. Construction men. Who's behind all that? Who's trying to louse things up? That's Mystery Number Four?"

Remo paused waiting for Chiun's wave to dismiss Mystery Number Four but no wave came.

"Well?"

"Are you quite done?" asked Chiun.

"Quite."

"All right. Then here is Mystery Number Five. If a man sets out on a journey and travels thousands of

153

miles to reach a place that is but a few miles away, he is doing what?"

"Going in the wrong direction," said Remo.

Chiun raised a finger. "Aaah, yes, but that is not the mystery. That is just a question. The mystery is why would a man who has done this and come to know it . . . why would that man go in the wrong direction again and again? That is the mystery."

"I assume all this blather has a point," Remo said.

"Yes. The point on your head between your ears. You are that man of Mystery Number Five. You travel and travel in the same direction always, searching for answers, and when you do not find them you keep traveling in the same direction."

"And?"

"And to unravel your mysteries—how many was it, four?—you must take another direction."

"Name one."

"Suppose your judgment of Mr. Fielding is wrong. Perhaps he is not victim but victimizer; perhaps not good but evil; perhaps he has seen what so many see about you—that you are a fool." Chiun chuckled. "After all, *that* is not one of the world's great mysteries."

"Okay. Say you're right. Why would he do this? If he is evil, what is he gaining by doing good?"

"And again I say do not jump from false opinions to empty conclusions without stopping to breathe. And sometimes to think."

"Are you saying that maybe Fielding has a scheme to do evil?"

"Aha. Sunrise comes at last, even after the darkest night."

"Why would he do that?"

"Of all the mysteries, the human heart is the most

unfathomable. It is many billions of mysteries for which there are never solutions."

Remo plopped back on the couch and closed his eyes as if to puzzle that one through.

"How American. There is never a solution so now you will weary yourself trying to find a solution. Better you take up one of those things your people call sports, as when two fools try to hit each other with a ball that they hit with paddles. I watched it earlier today."

"They're not trying to hit each other. They're trying to hit the ball somewhere so that the other player can't hit it back."

"Why not just hit it over the fence?"

"That's not in the rules."

"The rules are stupid then," said Chiun. "And what does that pudgy boy with the long hair and the face of a blowfish mean by strutting around like a rooster after hitting a ball?"

"It's complicated," said Remo. He started to sit up to explain, then thought better of it. "It's tennis. I'll tell you about it next time."

"And another thing. Why do they love each other if they are competitors? It might be one thing for the men to love the pretty woman with the sturdy child-bearing legs and the ears despoiled by rings. But to play love games with each other, that is sick."

"They're not in love with each other," said Remo. "That's how they keep score."

"That's right. Lie to me because I am Korean. I just heard on television that the one with the blowfish face had a love game. Would Howard Cosell lie to me?"

"Not if he knew what was good for him." Remo sank back onto the couch and began to ponder the

155

Fielding mysteries. Let Chiun try to unravel the mysteries of tennis and its scoring. Each man has his own mysteries and sufficient unto the man . . . . That was from the bible. He remembered the bible. It had been frequently referred to at the old orphanage although the nuns discouraged the children from reading it, under the assumption that a god who peeked into bathrooms, thus requiring them to bathe with undergarments on, would not be capable of defending himself against the mind of an inquisitive eight-year-old. Such was the nature of faith, and the stronger the faith the stronger the mistrust and misapprehension that it appeared to be based upon.

Was his faith in Fielding just that? Or was it just a suspicion of Chiun's?

Never mind. He would soon know. Fielding's Mojave unveiling was tomorrow and Remo and Chiun would be there. That might provide the answer to all mysteries.

There was another thing Remo remembered Chiun once saying about mysteries. Some cannot be solved. But all can be outlived.

Remo would see.

There were others making plans to go to the Mojave too.

In all of America, there were but eight Ninja experts who were willing to put their training into practice and kill. This, Johnny "Deuce" Deussio found out, after surveying the biggest martial arts schools in the country, weeding his way through overweight truckdrivers hoping to be discovered by television, executives trying to work out their aggressions, purse-snatchers looking for a new tool to aid them in their advancement to full-fledged muggers.

156

He found eight, all instructors, all Orientals. Their average age was forty-two but this did not bother Deussio because he had read all he could about Ninja and found that it differed from the other martial arts by its emphasis on stealth and deception. Karate, kung-fu, judo, the rest, they took a man's strength and intensified it. Ninja was eclectic; it took pieces from all the disciplines, and just those pieces that did not require strength to be efficient.

Johnny Deuce looked at the eight men gathered in the study of his fortress mansion. They wore business suits and if they had had briefcases, they might have resembled a Japanese executive team out scouring the world to squander its nation's newfound wealth on racehorses and bad paintings.

Deussio knew the eight included Japanese and Chinese and at least one Korean, but as he looked at them sitting around him in the study, he felt ashamed to admit to himself that they did all look alike. Except for the one who had hazel eyes. His face was harder than the others; his eyes colder. It was the Korean and Deussio decided, this man has killed. The others? Maybe. At any rate, they were willing. But this one . . . he has blood on his hands and he likes it.

"You know what I want," said Deussio to them. "One man. I want him dead."

"Just one?" It was the Korean, speaking in a neat, flavored English.

"That's all. But an exceptional man."

"Still. Eight exceptional men to bring him down seems excessive," the Korean said.

Deussio nodded. "Maybe after you see this, you won't think so."

He nodded to Sally who flipped out the room lights

and turned on the movie projector. Deussio had cut the film and this part included only Remo dodging the bullets, climbing the drainpipe, and disposing of the marksman.

The lights came back on. Some of the men, Deussio noticed, licked their lips nervously. The Korean, the one with the hazel eyes, smiled.

"Very interesting technique," he allowed. "But a direct Ninja attack. Very easy to handle. Eight men for this job is precisely seven too many."

Deussio smiled. "Just call it my way of insuring success. Now that you've seen the film, are you all still in?" He looked around the room. Eight heads nodded in agreement. By God, they did all look alike, he decided.

"All right then. Five thousand dollars will be deposited in each of your accounts tomorrow morning. Another five thousand dollars each will be deposited upon successful completion of the . . . er, mission."

They nodded again, simultaneously, like little plaster dolls with heads that bobbed on springs.

The Korean said, "Where will we find this man? Who is he?"

"I don't know much about him. His name is Remo. He will be at this place tomorrow." He gave them Xerox copies of news clippings about Fielding's Wondergrain and its unveiling in the Mojave.

He gave them a moment to look at the clippings.

"When do we attack? Is that left to our discretion?" asked the Korean.

"The demonstration is set for seven P.M. The attack must begin precisely at eight P.M. Precisely," said Deussio. "Not one minute early, not one minute late."

The Korean stood up. "He is as good as dead."

"Since you are so sure of that," said Deussio, "I want you to head this team. That is not making judgments on any of you others; it's just that everything works more smoothly if one man is in charge."

The Korean nodded and looked around the room. There were no dissenters. Just seven inscrutable masks.

Deussio gave them airline tickets and watched them leave his study. He was satisfied.

Just as he had been satisfied the night before when he had met with six snipers who had been recruited from the ranks of mobdom and had showed them the film of Remo wiping out the three Ninja in the alley.

He had promised them each ten thousand dollars, appointed a leader, and stressed the necessity that the attack begin at eight P.M.

"Exactly eight o'clock. Exactly. You got that?"

Nods. Agreement. At least he could tell the men apart.

He did not tell the snipers that the Ninja would also be attacking Remo, just as he had not told the Ninja about the marksmen. Their minds should be on only one thing. Remo, their target, and that target was as good as dead.

If he went straight-line attack against the Ninja, the rifles would take him out. And if he went Eastern-style against the rifles, Deussio's eight Ninja men would get him.

And if some of the snipers or Ninja got wasted . . . well that was part of the risk in a high-risk business.

The important thing was this Remo dead. And after him the rest of Force X. High probability, Folcroft Sanitarium, Rye, New York.

But as the next day dawned, Deussio remembered his head in the toilet and decided that it would not do just to stay home and wait for the good news. He wanted to be in at the kill.

"Sally," he ordered, "we're going on a trip."

"Where we going?"

"The Mojave Desert. I hear it's swinging this time of year."

"Huh?"

CHAPTER FIFTEEN

The Mojave.

The sun and heat, like hammers to the head, numbed the senses. People stood around, eyes baked dry, seeing everything through shimmering waves of heat. At night, the same people would still see everything through wavering lines, but they would not even notice it, so quickly did the human body and brain adjust to its environment.

The two large tents had again been erected outside the chain-link fencing that surrounded the experimental planting area, and both tents were crowded now in early evening with press men, with agricultural representatives of foreign countries, and with just the merely curious.

No one paid particular attention to six men who seemed to lurk about the scene in a group, each carrying a cardboard tube that looked as if it might hold a chart or a map. When a reporter with too much to drink tried to engage one of the men in conversation, he was brushed off with: "Get out of here before I shove my foot up your ass."

People peered through the fence of the still-locked compound, hoping for a glimpse of what Fielding might have produced. But the sunscreen filter still stood over the planting area and nothing inside was visible except seating benches.

A string of limousines, Cadillacs and Lincolns, were parked in a long line leading to the tents, along with one Rolls-Royce which belonged to the delegate from India, who was complaining that parts of America were so beastly hot, what, that it was no wonder the national character was so defective.

"We understand, sir," said a reporter, "that your country is the only one which has made no effort to sign up for Mr. Fielding's miracle grain, if it is successful."

"That is correct," said the delegate smoothly. "We will first examine the results and then we will plan our future policy accordingly."

"It would have seemed," said the reporter, "that with your chronic food problem, your nation would have been first in line."

"We will not have policy dictated to us by imperialists. If we have a food problem, it is our own."

"It seems strange then," said the reporter who was very young, "that America is continually asked to supply your nation with food."

The Indian delegate turned and walked away haughtily. He did not have to be insulted.

The reporter looked after him, then saw standing next to him an aged Oriental, resplendent in a blue robe.

"Do not be confused, young man," said Chiun. "Indians are that way. Greedy and unappreciative."

"And your nation, sir?" asked the reporter, gently prying.

"His nation," said Remo quickly, "is America. Come, Little Father."

Out of hearing of the reporter, Chiun spat upon the sand floor of the tent. "Why did you tell that awful lie?"

"Because North Korea, where Sinanju is, is a Communist country. We don't have diplomatic relations with them. Tell that reporter you're from North Korea and your picture'll be on every front page tomorrow. Every reporter will want to know what you're doing here."

"And I will tell them. I am interested in the onward march of science."

"Fine," said Remo.

"And I am employed in a secret capacity by the United State government . . . ."

"Great," said Remo.

"To train assassins and to kill the enemies of the Great Emperor Smith, thus preserving the Constitution."

"Do that and Smith'll cut off the funds for Sinanju."

"Against my better judgment," said Chiun, "I will remain silent."

Chiun seemed to stop in mid-sentence. He was looking through the opening of the tent at a group of men.

"Those men have been watching you," said Chiun.

"What men?"

"The men you are going to alert by turning around like a weathervane, shouting 'what men?' The Korean and the other nondescripts inside the tent."

Remo moved casually around Chiun and took in the men at a glance. Eight of them, Orientals, in their thirties and forties. They seemed ill at ease as if the business suits they wore did not really belong to them.

"I don't know them," Remo said.

"It is enough that they know you."

"Maybe it's you they're after," said Remo. "Maybe they came looking for a pool game."

Chiun's answer was interrupted by a roar from the crowd, which surged forward toward the locked guarded gates. Remo saw that Fielding had just driven up in a pickup truck.

Reporters pressed toward him as he stepped down from the driver's seat.

"Well, Mr. Fielding, what about it? We going to see anything today?"

"Just a few minutes. Then you can see to your heart's content."

Fielding signaled for the uniformed guards to open the gates and as they did, he turned toward the crowd.

"I'd appreciate it if you would move inside and take seats on the benches," he said. "That way everyone will be able to see."

Escorted by the three guards, Fielding walked to the black pastic sunscreen and turned to face the rows of benches which were filling rapidly. The last arrivals were Remo and Chiun and the delegate from India who had found a tray of delicious canapés and had tarried for just a few more. He finally entered through the open gates, walked to the front bench, and forced his way onto it between two men, while mumbling about American inconsiderateness.

Remo and Chiun stood behind the last bench. Chiun's eyes ignored Fielding to rove the compound.

"It was in here," he whispered softly, "that Fielding disappeared?"

"Yes," said Remo.

"Very strange," said Chiun. Almost as strange, he thought, as the six men holding cardboard tubes who had taken up positions outside the chain-link fence and were looking in. And almost as strange as the Korean and the seven other Orientals who now stood together in a corner of the compound, their eyes fixed on Remo. For a moment, the eyes of the younger Korean met Chiun's but the younger man looked quickly away.

Fielding cleared his throat, looked over the crowd, and intoned: "Ladies and gentlemen, I believe this may be one of the greatest days in the history of civilized man."

The Indian delegate snickered, while sucking a small lump of caviar from between his front teeth.

Fielding turned and with a wave of his hand signaled to the guards. They lifted the front edge of the plastic sunscreen, pulled it up, and then began hauling it toward the back of the planting area.

As the dying afternoon sun hit and glinted gold on the high healthy field of wheat, the crowd released one large collective breath. "Ooooooooh."

And there in the back was rice and barley and next to the wheat were soybeans.

"The fruits of my miracle process," Fielding shouted, waving a hand dramatically toward the field of food.

The audience applauded. There were cheers. The Indian delegate used the edge of his right thumbnail to pick a piece of cracker from between two back teeth.

The applause continued and swelled and it took

165

Fielding repeated shouts of "gentlemen" to quiet down the audience.

"It is my intention that this process will be used— virtually at cost—in any country which desires it. Wondergrain will be provided on a first-come, first-served basis. I have warehouses now filled with seed and it will be available for the nations of the world." He glanced at his watch. "It is now twenty after seven. I would suggest that you gentlemen inspect this crop. Take samples if you wish, but, please, only small samples since there are many of you and this is, after all, only a small field. In thirty minutes, let us reassemble inside the tents. I have representatives there who will meet with those delegates of any nations wishing to sign up for the Wondergrain process, and I will also be able to answer any press questions too. Please keep to the walkways through the field so the crop is not trampled underfoot. Thank you."

Fielding nodded and the reporters sprinted for the wooden walkways that divided the field into four sections. They grabbed up small handfuls of samples. Behind them, the other delegates began lining up to walk through the fields. The Indian delegate walked straight ahead, ignoring the wooden walkway, through the waist-high wheat, trampling it underfoot, grabbing samples to stuff into his briefcase. He turned and smiled. Back in the rear of the line he saw the French ambassador. How pleasant. The French ambassador was a Parisian, someone with whom he could honestly discuss the crassness and crudity of Americans.

Remo and Chiun watched and were watched.

"What do you think, Chiun?" asked Remo.

"I think there is a strange smell in this place. It smells like a factory."

Remo sniffed the air. The faint smell from before was there again. He was able to pin it down closer now; it was the scent of machine oil.

"I think you're right," said Remo.

"I know I am right," said Chiun. "I also know something else."

"What's that?"

"You are going to be attacked."

Remo looked down at Chiun, then his eye caught a motion off to the side. He saw a lone Cadillac limousine tooling its way down through the sand toward the front of the line. Behind the wheel was a face Remo recognized, even though the man now wore dark glasses and a hat, and the last time Remo had seen him he was wearing a toilet bowl. Johnny Deuce. Now what was he doing here?

Remo looked back on Chiun.

"An attack? On us?" said Remo.

"On you," corrected Chiun. "The Korean and the others. Those men outside the fence with their little cardboard tubes. Their eyes have all been on you and they are moving leadenly, like men on their way to deal with death."

"Hmmm," said Remo. "What should we do?"

Chiun shrugged. "Do what you like. It is no concern of mine."

"I thought we were coequal partners."

"Ah, yes. But that is in official assignments. If you go getting yourself into trouble on your own, you can't keep expecting me to help you."

"How many are there?" asked Remo.

"Fourteen. The eight Orientals. The six with the tubes."

"For fourteen, I don't need you."

"I certainly hope not."

Fielding was now leading the way to the twin tents outside the gates and the crowd was falling in line behind him, slowing down, unable to fit all at once through the gates.

As the Indian ambassador passed Chiun, he nodded curtly to the old man. "Gross, these Americans, what? How like them to try to sell this process which should rightly belong to all mankind."

"They pay their bills on time. They manage to feed themselves," said Chiun. "But don't worry. Wait long enough and they will give you this seed for free as they always do. They have a large stake in keeping you people alive."

"Oh," sniffed the Indian. "And what might that be?"

"You make them look good," said Chiun.

The Indian snorted and moved away from Chiun.

Remo was thinking about the smell of oil, fainter now with the powdered sand kicked up by so many feet, drifting through the air. The compound was almost empty. The fields of grain had been denuded by the sample pickers and had returned to the bare sand it had been only weeks before. The sunscreen was rolled up against the back fence and looking in over it, at Remo, was a hard-faced man carrying his cardboard tube. The man glanced at his watch.

"What do you think they've got in those tubes?" asked Remo.

"I do not think they are carrying flutes to play the music for the party."

Remo and Chiun turned toward the tents. The last of the crowd was disappearing through the door openings in the canvas, and now standing before them, blocking their way through the gates, were the eight Orientals.

They stood in a line across the gate and at a signal from the one with hazel eyes, they began to peel off their suits to reveal Ninja black combat suits.

"They are going to attack you with Ninja and the men with guns are going to attack you Western," said Chiun.

"Don't tell me your problems," said Remo. "You already said you were out of it."

"You are not good enough to stand against such an attack," said Chiun.

"'S all right," said Remo. "I've got to do everything around here anyway. It's not like I had a coequal partner or anything. But it's just me and my employee. And you know how hired help is these days."

"That is vileness unequaled by anything you have said before."

The Korean in the Ninja uniform spoke to Chiun. "Away, old man. We have no quarrel with you."

"I quarrel with your continued existence," said Chiun.

"It's your funeral, old man," the Korean said, glancing at his watch. Behind him, Remo heard a cardboard tube being ripped open and he turned to watch the six men around the outside of the fence pull out rifles.

"Eight o'clock," the Korean yelled. "Attack."

"Work the inside, Little Father," said Remo.

"Of course. I get all the dirty work," said Chiun.

The man at the far end of the compound was just raising his rifle to his shoulder as Remo and Chiun moved toward the eight Ninja men. The Orientals ignored Chiun and moved toward Remo but Chiun passed before Remo, moving from the left to the right, pulling in upon himself the force of the eight men, collapsing with it, and opening a gap that Remo darted through. The Ninja noticed Remo was gone only when

169

they looked for him, but when they tried to follow him through the gates, they found them blocked by Chiun, his arms spread wide, his voice intoning in Korean:

"The Master of Sinanju bids you die."

The six men outside the fence saw nothing but a pile of bodies. Where the hell was the white man? Fred Felice of Chicago was nearest the mass pileup, but the wire of the fence was in his way and he moved his head to see more clearly. Then the wire of the fence was no longer in his way as his head went through the fence like a hard-boiled egg being slammed through a wire slicer. He didn't last long enough to scream.

The next man screamed.

Remo reached him by moving crablike, skittering, remembering the lessons—the hour after hour of running at top speed along wet toilet tissue and being lectured by Chiun if he should so much as wrinkle the paper—and by the time he reached Anthony Abominale of Detroit, Abominale was just turning toward him. He shouted, then the shout turned into a scream that drowned in his throat on the blood that leaked into it from his shattered skull.

The shout brought the eyes of the other marksmen toward Remo.

"There he is. There he is." Bullets started pinging as the riflemen fired shot after shot from automatic clips. Remo kept moving, seeming to travel back and forth, seeming to take only one step forward and two steps back, but still moving like a slow wave of water toward the corner of the compound where another man waited, firing point blank. He was lucky. He was able to squeeze the trigger one last time. He was unlucky in that the rifle barrel was in his mouth when the gun went off.

170

As he moved, Remo glanced over his shoulder. The Ninja battle had moved into the center of the compound and all he could see of Chiun was an occasional flash of blue robe. Well. Nothing to worry about. There were only eight of them.

Remo went over the fence of the compound to come up upon the fourth man, then took him by vaulting back over the fence and with his feet driving the man's skull and spine deep down into his shoulders.

The fifth man got off two shots more before his intestines were ruptured with his own gun butt and the sixth dropped his weapon and ran but got only two steps before his face was buried deep in sand and he inhaled deep, sucked in the deadly grains, twitched once, and was still.

Then Remo was back at the front of the compound and running away from the tents through the dusk. A crowd had come out of the tents, attracted by the gunshots, and Remo moved silently past them, so quickly most did not even notice anyone passing. Then Remo was at the Cadillac which sat, motor idling, with Johnny Deussio behind the wheel.

Remo jerked open the door without bothering to depress the door-handle button.

Deussio looked at him in surprise that turned to fright, then to horror.

"Hiya," said Remo. "I almost didn't recognize you. You're not wearing your toilet."

"What are you going to do?"

"How many guesses you need?"

"Okay. Okay. But tell me. You really are a force fighting crime in this country, aren't you? Just tell me if I'm right."

"You're right. But don't look on us as a force. Look on us as a CURE."

And then Remo cured Johnny Deuce of life.

He did not wait for the autopsy. Instead he was back, moving through the crowds of people into the compound. Ahead he saw only motionlessness and as he grew nearer a mound of bodies. But no Chiun. He raced forward faster and as he neared the bodies, he caught a glimpse of the blue robes and he heard Chiun say, "Is it all right to come out?"

"Well, of course it's all right to come out."

Like a dolphin rising from water, Chiun moved up, seemingly unwrinkled, out of the mass of the dead, and Remo took his arm and walked him away, ignoring the crowds beginning to cluster around them.

"Why of course?" asked Chiun. "You play your games and those silly men are firing bullets all over and you think that one might not hit me? Do you think coequal partners are that easy to find? Particularly one who takes care of eight enemies while you are fooling around with only six?"

"Seven," said Remo. "I found another one over there in the car."

"Still. It is not eight."

A reporter clapped Chiun on the shoulder. "What happened? What happened? What's going on here?"

"Those men tried to overthrow the United States Constitution, but they did not reckon with the wiles and skill of the Master of Sinanju and his assistant," said Chiun. "They did not . . . ."

"Some kind of gang war," interrupted Remo. "These guys in here; those guys out there. The guy behind it is over in that Cadillac." He pointed to Johnny Deuce's car. "Talk to him."

Remo moved backwards with Chiun toward the far corner of the compound, out of the reach of the tent lights in the suddenly accumulated night darkness, and then he felt the sand under his feet and for a moment, it did not seem sandy enough.

"Chiun, what about this sand?"

"The feel is wrong," said Chiun. "Why do you think I worried about being hit by a bullet? I could not move right."

Remo sniffed. "Is that oil?"

Chiun nodded. "I have taken many breaths. Even your deserts smell in this country."

Remo rubbed his toe in the sand. The consistency underfoot did not feel right. He spun on his right foot, pushing off with his left, corkscrewing his right foot into the sand, and then stopped.

"Chiun, it's metal." He moved his leg around. His foot rested on a large metal plate. Through the thin leather soles of his Italian loafers, he felt small holes in the plate.

Remo pulled his right leg from the sand like a person yanking a toe from a too-hot bath.

"Chiun. I've got it."

"Is it contagious?"

"Don't be funny. The Wondergrain. It's a fake. Fielding's got an underground compartment here. The grain doesn't grow here. It's pushed up from underneath the sand. That's why those construction men were killed. They knew. They knew."

"And you have solved the riddle."

"This time, yes. The radioactive warehouse. This bastard's going to peddle radioactive grain and make farmland all over the world worthless. It'll make every famine the world ever had look like a picnic." He looked down at the sand, more in sorrow than in surprise. "I think it's time to talk to Fielding."

They moved through the crowd and then heard it—the whoop, whoop, whoop of an ambulance.

"Little late for an ambulance, Little Father," said Remo.

The ambulance rushed up toward the tent, kicking up sand sprays from its wheels and two men jumped from the back carrying a stretcher.

"What's going on?" Remo asked a reporter.

"Fielding. He collapsed."

Remo and Chiun passed through the crowd as if it were not there. As Fielding was being put on the stretcher, Remo leaned over to him and said:

"Fielding, I know. I know the whole scheme."

Fielding's face was chalky white, his lips almost violet under the harsh overhead light. The lips split into a thin smile as his unfocused eyes searched out Remo. "They're all bugs. Bugs. And now the bugs are all going to die. And I did it." His eyes closed again and the ambulance attendants carried him away.

CHAPTER SIXTEEN

"It couldn't be worse." Smith's voice sounded as forlorn and sour as his words.

"I don't know why. Just get rid of the radioactive seeds."

"They're gone," said Smith. "They've been moved from the Denver storage depot and we haven't yet been able to trace them. But we think they're probably someplace overseas."

"All right," said Remo. "Then just let the government brand the Fielding process as a hoax."

"That's the problem. That lunatic public relations company that Fielding's got, they're already out spreading the word that powerful government forces are trying to stop Fielding from feeding the world. If the government acts now, America'll wind up being labeled anti-human."

"Well, I've got a solution," said Remo.

"What's that?"

"Just let the seed get out and get planted around the world. And then there won't be anybody left to label us anti-human."

"I knew I could count on you for clear thinking," said Smith, his voice dripping ice. "Thank you."

"You're welcome," said Remo. "Call anytime."

After he hung up the phone, Chiun said, "You do not feel as good as you try to sound."

"It'll pass."

"No, it won't. You feel you have been made a fool of by Fielding and now people may suffer because of it."

"Maybe," Remo conceded.

"And you do not know what to do about it. Fielding is dying; you cannot threaten to kill him unless he tells the truth, because he just will not care."

"Something like that," Remo said. He looked out the window over the city of Denver. "I guess it's because Smitty feels so bad. You know, I could never tell him but I kind of respect him. He's got a tough job and he does it well. I'd like to help him out."

"Bah," said Chiun. "Emperors come and emperors go. You and I should go to Persia. There assassins are appreciated."

Remo shook his head, still looking at the skyline. "I'm an American, Chiun. I belong here."

"You are the heir to the title of Sinanju. You belong where your profession takes you."

"That's easy for you to say," said Remo. "I just don't want to leave Smith and CURE."

"And what of your coequal partner? Does my opinion count for nothing?"

"No, you're on the team too."

"All right. It is agreed."

"Wait a minute. Wait a minute. What is agreed?"

"It is agreed that I will solve this little problem for you. And in the future, you and Emperor Smith alone will not determine the assignments. I will have something to say about what you and I do."

"Chiun, did you ever do anything for anybody without extracting a price for it?" asked Remo.

"I am not the Salvation Army."

"What makes you think you can solve this problem?"

"Why not?" asked Chiun. "I am the Master of Sinanju."

James Orayo Fielding had only brief periods of consciousness now. The leukemia that was eating him up would win. It might be hours. It might be days. But the fight was over. Fielding was doomed.

Because of this, the doctors did not make any plans to operate or to minister to Fielding around the clock. Despite the fact that he was dying, he seemed to be happy, lying in his hospital bed, his face wreathed in smiles.

Until that afternoon when the aged Oriental appeared before him and offered to kiss his feet.

"Who are you?" asked Fielding softly of the ancient man in the light blue robe who stood at the foot of his bed.

"Just a humble man who has come to bring you the thanks of all mankind," said Chiun. "Already my poor village has been saved through your wonderful genius."

Fielding's eyes narrowed and for the first time in twenty-four hours, the smile passed from his face.

"But how?"

"Oh, you did not have all the process. You were very

close," Chiun said, "but you missed one thing. The chemicals you put into the grain, they could be very dangerous, but we found the thing to render them harmless."

As Fielding's face lengthened, Chiun went on.

"Salt," he said. "Common salt. Found everywhere. Seeded into the soil with your grain, it makes plants grow, not in weeks, but in only days. And it has no bad effects. Like that bomb long ago in Japan. Look!"

Chiun opened his hand and lowered it to show Fielding his palm. In it rested a solitary seed. From his other hand, Chiun sprinkled some white grains on the seed. "Salt," he explained.

He closed the hand and then opened it again. The seed had already begun to sprout. A tiny shoot rose from the top of it.

"It takes now only moments," said Chiun. He closed his hand again. When he reopened it, a few seconds later, the shoot had grown. It was now an inch tall, sprouting above the seed.

"All the world will sing your praises," said Chiun. "You will feed the world instantly. Never again will there be hunger because of you."

He bowed deeply at the foot of Fielding's bed and then backed from the room, as if leaving the presence of a king.

Fielding's mouth tried to move. Salt. Just common salt could make his process work. Because of him, the buggy humans would eat happily ever after. He had failed. His monument that was to be carved from the deaths of billions had failed . . . unless . . . .

The public relations firm of Feldman, O'Connor and the late Mr. Jordan had no trouble getting the press to meet in Fielding's hospital room for a major press conference at six o'clock that night. After all, Fielding was a world-famous figure. His every move was news.

Chiun and Remo sat in their hotel room watching on television, as James Orayo Fielding told the reporters that his Wondergrain process was a hoax.

"Just a prank," he said, "but now I find that it can be very dangerous. The radioactivity in the seeds could hurt the bugs . . . er, that is the people who come in contact with it. I am ordering the ships that were carrying this seed overseas for distribution to dump their cargo instantly to protect the people of the world from harm."

Remo watched on the television, then turned to Chiun.

"All right. How'd you do it?"

"Shhhh," said Chiun. "I am listening to the news."

After the press conference, the newscaster reported that the first comment on Fielding's announcement had just been received from the government of India. While India had not bid on the food process, it might be interested in taking the radioactive waste off Fielding's hands—at no charge, of course—for further research into potential military uses of it. Booby traps, the newscaster said.

When the news show had turned safely to weather and sports, Remo asked again: "How'd you do it?"

"I reasoned with him."

Remo stood up. "That's no answer." He walked around the room, stalking, awaiting another word from Chiun. None came. Remo went to the window and looked out again. His hand came to rest on the window-sill and brushed against something.

He picked it up.

"And what is this plastic plant doing here?" he asked.

"It is a gift for you. To remind you of the everlasting goodness of your Mr. Fielding. May the bugs feast forever on his body."

BLOCKBUSTER FICTION FROM PINNACLE BOOKS!

THE FINAL VOYAGE OF THE S.S.N. SKATE   (17-157, $3.95)
by Stephen Cassell
The "leper" of the U.S. Pacific Fleet, SSN 578 nuclear attack sub SKATE, has one final mission to perform—an impossible act of piracy that will pit the underwater deathtrap and its inexperienced crew against the combined might of the Soviet Navy's finest!

QUEENS GATE RECKONING   (17-164, $3.95)
by Lewis Purdue
Only a wounded CIA operative and a defecting Soviet ballerina stand in the way of a vast consortium of treason that speeds toward the hour of mankind's ultimate reckoning! From the best-selling author of THE LINZ TESTAMENT.

FAREWELL TO RUSSIA   (17-165, $4.50)
by Richard Hugo
A KGB agent must race against time to infiltrate the confines of U.S. nuclear technology after a terrifying accident threatens to unleash unmitigated devastation!

THE NICODEMUS CODE   (17-133, $3.95)
by Graham N. Smith and Donna Smith
A two-thousand-year-old parchment has been unearthed, unleashing a terrifying conspiracy unlike any the world has previously known, one that threatens the life of the Pope himself, and the ultimate destruction of Christianity!

Available wherever paperbacks are sold, or order direct from the Publisher. Send cover price plus 50¢ per copy for mailing and handling to Pinnacle Books, Dept. 17-237, 475 Park Avenue South, New York, N.Y. 10016. Residents of New York, New Jersey and Pennsylvania must include sales tax. DO NOT SEND CASH.

CRITICALLY ACCLAIMED MYSTERIES
FROM ED MCBAIN AND PINNACLE BOOKS!

THE EXECUTIONER
by Don Pendleton